DESSERTS AND DECEPTION

A MARGOT DURAND COZY MYSTERY

DANIELLE COLLINS

FAIRFIELD PUBLISHING

THANK you so much for buying my book. I am excited to share my stories with you and hope that you are just as thrilled to read them.

If you would like to know about all my new releases and have the opportunity to get free books, make sure you sign up for our Cozy Mystery Newsletter.

FairfieldPublishing.com/cozy-newsletter

CHAPTER 1

MARGOT DURAND DRUMMED her fingers on the steering wheel as she maneuvered her car into position in the airport pickup zone. It was growing dark and she hoped that Tamera's flight hadn't been delayed. Margot hadn't thought to check it before she left North Bank for Ronald Reagan Airport near Washington, D.C.

The sound of classical music wound through her scattered thoughts. She was tired. It had been an early morning—a baker's morning, as she liked to call them—and she was considering, once again, hiring an assistant. She had the overhead and the fact was, if she *did* hire someone competent enough, her mornings wouldn't have to be quite so early. But the fact of the matter was that she was a tough boss to work for. She demanded perfection of herself and any assistant would have to be strong enough to put up with that.

Spotting Tamera, she pulled her car to the curb and

hopped out, thoughts of hiring an assistant pushed to the back of her mind as she embraced her best friend.

"You're back!"

Tamera laughed and pulled back to look at Margot. "You look tired."

"And you look tan."

Tamera positively glowed, her smile widening as her blush deepened. "We spent quite a bit of time on the beach."

"Good for you," Margot said. She leaned down and picked up her friend's suitcase.

"I can get that."

"Nonsense," Margot said, popping the trunk of the car. "Hop on in. It's way too hot out here."

Tamera agreed and slipped into the passenger's seat as Margot made her way back behind the wheel. She pulled into traffic and soon they were heading down 395 toward North Bank, Virginia, and their small, historical hometown.

"Gosh, it's good to be back."

"You know, some people actually prefer vacations to real life." Margot laughed at the look her friend gave her.

"I love my store and being away from the Craft Boutique for two weeks just about killed me." Tamera sighed. "Speaking of, can we stop by?"

Margot snuck a glance at her friend. "You're not serious."

"I am."

"You just got back!"

"And my store has been closed for two weeks. *Two* whole weeks, Marg. That's a long time. I...I miss it."

Margot couldn't help her grin. "I suppose I understand. I don't remember the last time I left the *Pâtisserie* for that long." *Or at all.* She added the need for a vacation to her mental to-do list.

An image of the *The Parisian Pâtisserie* filled Margot's mind. Her little shop sat along a row of others like it, their back doors looking out over the Potomac River and their entrances facing the main, cobbled street of North Bank.

Margot's bakery boasted all the goodness of a French bakery mixed with traditional American baked goods to please everyone. The shop's pale yellow exterior fit in with the bright colors of the other shops, but inside, she'd decorated with an eye toward a true French bakery as best she could.

It would be difficult to leave her shop for that long, just as it would be difficult to hire someone else.

"What's on your mind, friend?" Tamera's softly asked question broke into Margot's thoughts.

"Sorry. I just...I had lunch with Adam the other day and—"

"You *did*, did you?"

Margot sent her friend a look. "It was just lunch. We do that all the time."

"Ever since you and he became reacquainted at the end of spring, you've been seeing much more of one another. I've noticed. That's all."

Margot thought of the case her friend was talking of. Her niece, Taylor, had been accused of murdering a young

4

man who'd been new to town. She shivered just at the memories.

"We're *friends*," she said, emphasizing the word, "and friends have lunch together now and again."

"All I'm saying is don't close yourself off to...more."

Margot wasn't even going to give Tamera the courtesy of answering that. "Anyway, he said that I should consider hiring someone to help me at the bakery."

"What happened to Rosie?"

"Oh, no, I've still got Rosie." Margot smiled. "I'll never let her go."

"She's like a rare jewel, that's for sure," Tamera agreed.

"He was saying for the baking part."

"Oh." Margot caught Tamera's nod out of the corner of her eye. "But that's a pretty personal thing. Right? I mean...it means sharing your recipes and stuff like that."

"Yes." Margot had thought through all of these things multiple times. "I can't get away from the fact that it would be great to have someone to fall back on. A way that I could keep from closing the shop every time I get sick or want to take a day off."

"I can't believe you've made it this long without help."

"You have."

"Yes." Tamera nodded. "But I have a different clientele. And my stock keeps."

"True. But I did have help at one point. You remember Casey, right? But then she went off to grad school and I slipped back into old habits. Thankfully, my ability to pay the bills doesn't revolve around the bakery, but still..." The money she'd received when her husband had been killed in the line of duty, or so the reports said, was well invested. She would be fine to retire any moment she wanted to, but the bakery was something special to her. More than a paycheck, it was a passion.

"I understand. But I'm inclined to agree with Secret Agent Man."

"Don't call him that," Margot said with a smile.

"He's got a point. And think of it this way, you're not just helping yourself, you're helping someone else."

Margot let go of the breath she'd been holding and exited the freeway. Turning toward town, she thought through what her friend had said. It was a good point. There were plenty of people out there who needed jobs. Maybe she was being selfish by not hiring someone.

"Good point, Tam. Maybe it's time to start looking for the right person to hire." She turned onto a side street.

"Hey, where are we going? You promised to take me to my shop!"

"And I will," Margot said, flashing her a devious smile, "but first we're stopping by Claytons."

Tamera let out a girlish giggle. "I have *missed* Claytons. Let's go!"

Margot relaxed back into her seat, finally feeling some peace in her heart. Two of her good friends thought hiring someone was a good idea, and she couldn't ignore that. But now it was time to put thoughts of work aside and focus on what was truly important in this moment.

Ice cream.

"THAT WAS SO GOOD," Tamera said, clutching at her flat stomach. "I'm going to have to take an extra-long run in the morning."

"Does that mean I get to take you *home* now? To that handsome husband of yours?"

Tamera laughed. "Not a chance. To my shop we go."

Margot shook her head but put the car in gear, turning down the street that would take them toward the Craft Boutique.

"Did you tell Hubby you wouldn't be home right away?"

"Yep," Tamera said, the smile evident even in one word. "He actually came back two days ago and will be working late. I assume he'll be getting home about the time I do."

"He's been working a lot, huh?"

"He's a trial lawyer in D.C. What do you expect?"

Her friend's words were laced with something Margot couldn't put her finger on. "How was the vacation?"

"Perfect. No, better than perfect. It was so relaxing. Marg, it's what I always imagined a honeymoon could be."

"So it was worth the wait?"

Tamera laughed, the sound low and booming in the small car. "In more ways than one. Part of me wishes I could have taken the time off when we first got married. I mean, the three days in Nantucket were great right after the wedding, but *this* was the honeymoon I had wanted. George seemed to love it too."

Margot remembered her friend's absence at the end of spring that year. She'd missed almost all of the controversy surrounding Taylor's visit, but thankfully, she'd come back in time to meet Margot's sister Renee.

Margot pulled her car into a parking space in front of the boutique, thankful for the later hour, which meant almost no traffic on Front Street.

"You're finally back, eh?"

Margot nearly jumped out of her skin. "Mrs. Henderson. I didn't see you there."

The older woman stood with one hand shoved into the pocket of her jeans and the other wrapped tightly around a leash, at the end of which was a portly corgi. Its tail wagged even as the woman frowned at Tamera and Margot.

"Hello, Phyllis," Tamera said, smiling as if Phyllis Henderson's frown was anything but. "Nice night for a walk, eh?"

The woman grunted and kept walking. Margot watched her go, shaking her head. "I swear she does nothing but spy on people."

"She runs The Pet Depot, silly," Tamera said with a grin.

"You I know what I mean."

"I do. But give her a break. She lives above the shop and has nothing else to do."

Margot nodded in agreement and followed Tamera to the door.

"Hello, beautiful," Tamera whispered to the door.

"You've officially lost it."

"For the longest time, I didn't have anything else, Marg."

"But now you've got George. Does he know of this love affair you have going with your boutique?"

Tamera shot her a look, barely indiscernible in the darkness. "He knows. And he's slowly helping me let go."

Margot followed her friend's laughter into the shop, the scents of paper, scented candles, and an odd scent she couldn't place greeting them.

"Does it...smell strange to you?"

Tamera sniffed. "Maybe a little. It has been closed for two weeks. That's a long time."

"True."

"I've got to get to the back of the shop to get the lights. Give me a second."

Margot watched her friend pick her way through the darkened shop, the only light coming from a streetlight almost a block down. She was about to pull out her phone to turn on the flashlight when Tamera shrieked.

"Tamera!" Margot called out. She rushed toward the sound but her foot caught on a table, almost sending it toppling over. "*Oof.* Tamera, what is it?"

"Oh my gosh, Marg. I think...I...I..."

"What's wrong?" Margot was almost to the back of the shop now.

"I think it's a body."

Margot's blood ran cold. "What?"

Just as she reached the back of the shop, the lights came on to show Tamera standing over a body, face down on the floor. It was a man dressed in khaki shorts and wearing a Hawaiian print shirt. A dark brown fedora was off to the side of his head, turned upside-down. Margot noted smudges of what looked like—was it makeup?—on the inside rim.

Without thought, Margot knelt next to the man and felt for a pulse, pressing down nausea as she did. His skin was cold and firm to the touch.

"Tam, you need to call the police. Now!" Margot stood back up, wrapping her arms around herself.

There was no doubt. The man was dead.

CHAPTER 2

"Margot Durand," a deep voice said behind her. "Fancy meeting you here."

She turned to see Detective Adam Eastwood. He wore running shorts and a t-shirt that fit him much too well. She swallowed and forced her eyes from his muscled chest to meet his intent stare.

"Adam," she gasped.

"I hear you found a body?" There was sweat on his shirt and dotting his brow. Had he been on a run? "Margot?"

She blinked. Her thoughts were scattered and she couldn't get the picture of the man lying dead on the floor out of her mind.

"Y-yes."

"Hey," Adam said, stepping closer, "it's going to be all right. I'm here now."

His words were comforting—almost too much so—

and she suddenly felt self-conscious, looking to where Tamera stood talking to another officer.

"Want to tell me what happened?"

She was surprised to see he had a notepad in his hand and was ready to get down to business. As the town's resident detective, she knew he had a job to do and she was part of that job. Nodding, she explained exactly what had happened, ending with the fact that she'd felt for a pulse but, finding none, had Tamera call the police.

"Good, good." He scribbled some notes and then looked up at her. "Did you recognize the man at all?"

"No." She shook her head. "But I didn't get a good look. I almost turned him over but when I didn't feel a pulse, I figured I shouldn't disturb the crime scene."

"Good thinking." He wrote some more. "And Tamera, you said you'd just picked her up?"

"Yes. Well, we got ice cream first."

"Claytons?" His easy grin told her he was trying to calm her down.

"It's the only place to go for ice cream, really."

"Agreed. And then you came here? Did you see anyone?"

"No— Oh, well, we saw Mrs. Henderson walking a dog."

"Phyllis?"

"Yeah."

"Noted." He looked up just as Margot heard a familiar voice. "Looks like George is here."

Margot turned to see George with his arms around Tamera. She was crying into his chest and, for a moment,

Margot envied her—if only just a little. There had been a time when Margot had cried like that into Julian's chest, but that had been in the past.

"Why don't we go over there?" Adam suggested, as if sensing her mood.

They walked over just as the EMTs were bringing out the body. It looked as if one of them hadn't zipped up the body bag all the way and the stiff wind from the Potomac yanked the flap back and forth.

George's gasp drew everyone's attention.

"That's Mark!"

Adam rounded on George with wide eyes. "You *know* the victim?"

George stammered, unable to take his eyes from the body.

"Hold on, guys," Adam instructed. Then, turning to Margot and Tamera, he said, "You may want to look away. George, can you take a quick look? To verify you know the victim?"

Looking grim, George took a step toward the body. Before Margot could turn her head, one of the EMTs pulled back the flap and exposed the man's face. It seared into her memory and she gasped, pulling her gaze away.

"Tell me this isn't happening," Tamera said, Margot coming to her side. "Tell me I didn't just find a dead body in my craft shop."

Margot wanted to be able to tell her friend that, but the truth was it *had* happened. She wrapped her arm around Tamera and pulled her close, risking a glance back toward where George stood. From her perspective, she

DANIELLE COLLINS

could just see the lines on his forehead deepen. His nod to Adam told her all she needed to know. George *did* know the victim. But how?

"Marg, can we go? I just...I don't want to be here."

Margot swallowed down her curiosity. It wasn't so much that she wanted to butt into Adam's investigation, but why had this man—whom George apparently knew—been found in Tamera's boutique? Margot almost felt responsible, though she knew that was foolish. She'd only been in charge of keeping a set of Tamera's keys and checking on the place every once in a while.

She'd just been in there...when was that? She thought back. Three days ago. Everything had seemed fine and there had *definitely not* been a body in there when she checked on the place in preparation for Tamera's homecoming.

"Marg?"

Margot blinked. Tamera had asked her a question. Right. "I'm sorry. I was...distracted. Um, let me ask Adam if we can go." Tamera gave a vague nod and wrapped her arms around herself.

Margot waited until the EMTs had gotten back in the ambulance before she approached Adam. He and George were in the middle of a conversation and she hated to interrupt, but she wasn't sure what else to do. She came up quietly, waiting.

"I don't know *how* he got in there—" George pointed to the boutique. "—or how he was killed. I mean...I don't even know how he would have gotten down to North Bank."

14

"Because you know he doesn't have a car?"

George shook his head and raked a hand through his greying hair. "The last I knew, he was staying in protective custody in D.C. awaiting the trial."

"Protective—" Adam sighed and now he ran a hand through his dark, short-cropped hair, mirroring George. "What can you tell me about his protection?"

"Not much. I'm part of a team of lawyers, Adam. I know what I'm focused on and that's about it." George shrugged. "More or less."

Margot saw Adam's eyes narrow and she had a feeling he didn't believe George—or had some doubts about what he was saying. Why? George wouldn't lie. And what was this about being on a team of lawyers? Margot's thoughts raced to catch up.

She knew George was a lawyer in D.C. and that he commuted from North Bank. It had to be a nasty commute, but Tamera insisted that he enjoyed the time on the metro and that it was a small sacrifice he was willing to pay in order to live in the less-hectic area of North Bank. But if George knew the victim *and* the victim had been under protective custody...that meant he was likely a witness in a case. Didn't it? But what case?

"Margot?" Adam's gentle voice accompanied his light touch to her arm and she jerked her mind to the present.

"Uh, Tamera—and I—were wondering if we can go. It's late and she's tired, understandably."

"Right." Adam looked at George then back at Margot. "George, why don't you go ahead and take your wife

15

home. I'll have more questions but they can wait until tomorrow."

George nodded and Margot could see him swallow. Was he nervous? Or just shaken by the night's events?

"Thanks," George said to Adam. "And thanks for picking up Tamera tonight," he said to Margot.

She offered him a tired smile as he turned and went to his wife. Her friend dissolved into her husband's arms and, for a brief moment, Margot felt the slight stab of jealousy again.

Pull yourself together, Margot. There's been a murder!

She blinked and the feelings were gone, replaced by the reality of what had happened that night.

"Hey," Adam said, coming to stand next to her and wrapping an arm around her shoulders. "You look tired yourself. Doing okay?"

She wasn't sure how to answer that. The image of the man's pale face still haunted her. But, more than that, she wanted to know who he was. What case had he been a witness for? His death was surely linked to that. Though Adam would know all of those things.

"I'll be all right. Just shaken."

"Understandable." He turned her to face him, letting his hands rest lightly on her arms just above her elbows. "Now why don't you go on home? Get some rest? I may have more questions tomorrow, but I can come by after the shop is open or…later. I could bring dinner."

His words didn't register at first, but then she lifted her gaze to his. He was giving her a look she couldn't quite decipher. But, the moment she thought she saw it, it was gone.

"Uh, sure. Tomorrow," she said, noncommittally.

"You're still considering hiring someone, right?"

She laughed. He was so insistent about it. "I'm considering it."

"Good. Now go home and sleep. Okay?"

She nodded.

"Do you want me to drop you? I could drive your car and finish my run on the way back to my place," he said with a laugh.

She shook her head. "You probably need to finish up here, I'm assuming. I'll be fine."

He nodded, holding her gaze again. She almost thought he would say something else, but instead, he dropped his hands, releasing her from their warmth and the connection to him.

He was right. She needed to get home and sleep.

Or see if she could find what case the man had been a witness for.

No! She reasoned with herself as she walked toward her car. She was *not* getting in the middle of this.

MARGOT LAY IN BED, staring up to the darkened ceiling that held shadows cast from the trees in front of the streetlight outside of her window. She should be sleeping, it was way past the time that she should have been in bed, but she couldn't fall asleep. Every time her eyes closed, the man's face floated before her.

At first it had been frightening, but the more she tried to push the face away and find sleep the more she began to reason through what she'd seen at the crime scene that night.

They hadn't been in the boutique long but she knew a few things for certain. The front door hadn't been broken into so the killer and victim had either broken in the back or had a key for either door. As far as she knew, only she, Tamera, and probably George had keys. It was possible the old landlord still had a pair too, but Tamera had bought the building outright with inheritance money after her father died. Had she changed the locks?

After mulling over that for far too long, Margot rolled onto her side and thought about what she could remember seeing.

They had walked through the darkened part of the shop. Tamera had gone ahead because she knew the way in the dark better than Margot. She had turned on the lights in the back and screamed—of course, because she'd seen the body. A natural reaction. Then…Margot had rushed to the back, nearly falling over a table leg, and seen the man.

Nothing was out of the ordinary in her memory. Now she considered how they'd found the man. He'd been face down when she went to search for a pulse and she suppressed a shudder at the memory of his cold skin. No pulse. No blood.

Odd. She wondered what the cause of death would be.

From what she'd seen of his back and then the brief—but still too long—look at his face, there hadn't been any trauma to report. Drugs? Poison?

Then there was the fedora. The temperature had been pushing ninety degrees even in the evenings most nights for the last week. There was no cause for a man to be wearing a fedora whatsoever, at least not at night. Then again, some men liked to wear hats all the time. Maybe he was like that?

Sighing, she rolled onto her other side. This was ridiculous. What was she going to do? Solve the murder from her bed at midnight? Unlikely. But there was something about the scene that had been off to her and she couldn't put her finger on it. Even now, as sleep began to take hold, she felt unsettled. She'd seen something—she knew it—but she had no way of knowing what it was.

Maybe she would remember in the morning. Maybe...

CHAPTER 3

THE SMELL of heavy sweetness laced the air as Margot pulled the last batch of walnut, chocolate chip cookies from the oven. She'd worked past her allotted morning time, feeling the strain of only a few hours of sleep, but she was finally done and she'd only had a few customers drawing her from the back. For once she was thankful for a quiet morning.

"Hello?" a rough voice called from the front.

Her smile slipped into place easily and she called out, "Be right there, Bentley!"

His lack of response was typical and she rushed to slide the cookies off the baking sheet so they wouldn't over bake. Then she cut an extra corner out of an *Oopsie*— what she called any baked good that didn't meet up to her standards for the shop—and added it to Bentley's usual order.

"Thought I'd fall asleep before you made it out here," he teased good-naturedly.

"How about an extra slice of a caramel pecan cinnamon roll and a cup of coffee on the house to make up for it?"

"You barely make me pay as it is. But I accept."

She grinned and slid the baked goods in front of him. "When am I going to get you to try something else?"

He took a bite, his eyes closing and some of the wrinkles smoothing out. "Never," he whispered.

She laughed, shaking her head. "You're set in your ways, aren't you, Mr. Lawyer?" Ever since she'd found out he used to be a trial lawyer in D.C., she hadn't let him forget she knew his past.

"Quite right, Detective."

She shook her head, taking his nickname in stride. Around the same time she'd found out about his past profession, she'd also helped solve a murder case and he'd taken to calling her Detective. Thankfully not around Adam—yet—but she had a feeling it was only a matter of time.

Her thoughts slipped to the night before. All of this talk about lawyers and detectives caused her curiosity to run wild, but she couldn't go there. That was Adam's job, not hers.

"Heard about the hubbub last night," Bentley said casually.

She stopped scrubbing the already-clean countertop and turned to look at him. "You did?"

"News travels fast in this town. Besides, Phyllis Henderson is best friends with Anita Mallord who lives two doors down from me in the senior living apartments.

Of course Phyllis had to come and see her last night and then *she* nearly knocked down my door to tell me about it. Police cars and a body wheeled out on a stretcher." He tossed his hands up and shook his head. "What is this town coming to?"

Margot wasn't sure what she could—or should—share about it all. Just as she was about to make a non-specific comment, the front door opened and Adam walked in. His hair still looked damp from his morning shower and she caught a whiff of his aftershave moments after his entrance. It smelled sweet and spicy.

"Adam," she said, surprised. For some reason, talking about last night with Bentley when he walked in somehow felt wrong. "What are you doing here?"

"I told you I was going to stop by," he said with an easy grin. "Hey, Bentley, how are the crosswords going?"

Bentley tossed up a hand. "Terrible. Atrocious. Abhorrent."

Adam grinned. "But you're still working on them, eh?"

"You betcha, boy. It improves my vocabulary."

"I'm sure it does. Hey, Margot," Adam said, turning toward her, "can we chat in the back?"

She nodded and led the way to the kitchen. The warmth of the oven filled the space, as did the scent of cookies and pastries, but Adam didn't seem to mind. He zeroed in on the *Oopsies* and helped himself after a glance for permission. She poured him a cup of coffee and then crossed her arms, leaning back against the counter.

"I thought you were coming around lunchtime? Or later?"

"Is now a bad time?" he asked around a mouthful of pastry.

"No, I just..." What? Was caught off guard thinking about the murder like a detective—again? "No. It's not a bad time."

"Good." He wiped his mouth with the napkin she handed him and then took a sip of the hot coffee, letting it wash away the sugar that no doubt coated his throat. "So, I've got to ask you some additional questions. That okay?"

"Of course." She wasn't sure why he looked so hesitant. This was part of his job, she knew that better than anyone. Last night would set the course of Adam's days from now until the culprit was arrested. Of anyone, she knew this better than most. Her late husband Julian had been a detective with the same precinct as Adam. She knew how it worked. Knew what his life would look like from here on out.

She was about to tell him as much when her cellphone rang. Sending him an apologetic look, she rushed to her small office and snatched her phone from the desk. She was about to silence it when she noticed it was Tamera. Considering the previous night, she decided to answer despite the fact she was making Adam wait.

Tamera was her friend and a fellow businesswoman in a small town. Adam would understand waiting for a few extra minutes.

"Hello?"

"Oh, thank God you answered!"

Tamera sounded frantic. Had she found another body?

The thought, as strange as it was, crossed Margot's mind but she pushed it away.

"Calm down, Tam. What's wrong?"

Tamera panted as if she'd run from somewhere. "I was," gasp, "just out on," gasp, "a run and I came back," she took a moment to swallow, "to find a message on my phone from George."

Though Margot had no idea what the message was about, she knew by Tamera's frantic gasping that it wasn't anything good.

"What is it? What did he say?"

"He's—" She gasped again, but this time it sounded more like a sob. "He's been arrested."

"What?!" Margot forgot the fact that that she was in her shop or that anyone else could hear her. Her shouted reply came from pure shock.

"I know." Tamera was crying now, the tears heavily lacing her voice. "I can't believe it. He couldn't tell me much, but I knew I had to call you."

"Arrested, not brought in for questioning?" she clarified.

"Arrested," Tamera all but wailed back.

Margot reasoned through all of the things that could have caused George to be arrested. She could only assume that it was in response to the murder, but he had helped identify the victim. That was hardly cause for being arrested, was it? It had to be something much worse.

"Please, help him Marg! You know Adam and—"

"Adam," Margot said out loud and heard the scrape of a ceramic mug on her metal countertops. He was out there right now in her kitchen. Had he come by because he already knew George was arrested? Was that the reason for his hesitance?

"Tam, I've got to go." She straightened and mentally prepared for a battle of wills with Adam. "But don't worry. I'll talk to Adam and call you back as soon as I hear anything. Okay?"

"Promise?"

"Promise. Now go take a shower, eat something, and try to calm down. It'll be all right."

It had to be, because Margot knew there was no way George Wells had killed anyone.

※

Margot walked back into the kitchen and stood at the counter, arms crossed and hip pressed against the cold metal side. Adam looked appropriately contrite but she waited, wanting to hear it from him.

"That was Tamera?"

She merely nodded.

"And she told you we arrested George this morning."

She nodded again.

"Okay, so maybe I should have led with that today. And don't keep nodding. Your silence throws me off."

She dropped her arms. "Why didn't you tell me? You know Tamera is my best friend."

"I was going to get there…eventually."

"Sure, after you ate all my pastries, drank all of my coffee, and I answered your questions. What was it going to be, 'Oh, by the way, Margot, we arrested George, bye'?" She raised an eyebrow and the corner of his lip inched upward.

"Actually, I was going to call you once I was in the safety of my car." He cracked a smile and she shook her head. "No, really, Margie, I was going to tell you."

He used his nickname for her and, though she'd once hated it, she had to admit she was used to it now and it had a softening effect on her.

"Then tell me what's going on. Why did you arrest George?"

He scrunched up his face like he did when he wanted to tell her something but couldn't because of protocol. She understood it, even if she disliked the fact that she couldn't get all of the information she needed from him. It sounded so awful, like she was using him merely for his role as detective, but that wasn't the case.

"All I can say is that there is a witness that places George at the craft boutique during or around the time of the victim's death and we couldn't verify his alibi."

"What?" Margot felt like the air in the shop had just disappeared. George had been seen at the boutique? Normally that wouldn't bet too strange, but Tamera hadn't even been back yet and he was there? But why?

"Wait, when was time of death?"

"We're still waiting on the final results from the medical examiner, but his initial assessment puts it at or around five last night."

"What? That seems unlikely."

"Why do you say that?"

Margot paced to the sink and poured herself a glass of water before answering. "It would still be light out at five. How would someone kill a person in broad daylight?"

"They were in the shop—"

"You don't really believe that, do you?"

He frowned, eyes narrowing. "What makes you think otherwise?"

"Last night when we came in, it was dark—really dark. I had just reached for my cell phone to turn on the flashlight app when Tamera walked through to the back to get the lights. Nothing was out of place. Nothing moved—at least I don't think so, or else she would have been tripped up. She knows that store like the back of her hand. So, no struggle. Besides, where was the blood? Then again, we don't know how he died…" She trailed off. Her gaze had gone to the window while she thought and only when Adam lightly touched her shoulder did she jolt back to the present.

"Hey, nice to have you back among the living."

She made a face at him. "I was thinking."

"And that's what worries me."

"What's that supposed to mean?"

His head tilted to the side. "Margot, you know how I feel about you putting yourself in the middle of dangerous situations and—"

"If George is the murderer, then you have him in custody." She folded her arms again and waited.

He rolled his eyes. "All right, so I don't think George did it either."

"I knew it! Then why did you arrest him?"

27

"Because my chief doesn't listen to gut feelings or the fact that George is a friend of a friend. He goes by facts— like George being at the scene of the crime apparently both times. When it allegedly happened and when the body was found."

"But he was coming to pick up his *wife!*"

Adam held up a hand as if to say, *I know, I know.* The facts didn't look good for George, but it was encouraging to hear that Adam was on her side. Not that she could really have a side at this point—merely the side of her friend.

"I do still have a few questions I need to ask you, if you'll cooperate?"

She cracked a smile. "For you, Detective Eastwood? Absolutely."

He seemed pleased by her reply and pulled out his notebook. "What can you tell me about George?"

The question, seemingly innocuous, meant so much more now that Margot knew he was in custody, but she tried to separate that from her thoughts and focus merely on the questions.

"I've been best friends with Tamera for over fifteen years. About a year ago, she signed up for one of my baking classes."

"I saw you offered those. I've wanted to join—I've always wanted to be able to bake." The genuine interest in Adam's eyes caught her off guard.

"Really?"

"Yeah." He shifted nervously and looked down at his notepad. "Sorry, where were we?"

A new image of Adam Eastwood formed in Margot's mind, but she refocused on the task at hand. "I often get clients from the D.C. area, being so close and all, and since I supplied pastries to a few well known parties, I would often get higher profile guests." She thought back to the night class she'd offered. There had been six students, all of differing ages, genders, and interests. It had been a fun class. With the hint of a smile still on her lips, she continued. "George was part of that class. When we did introductions and he said he was a lawyer in D.C., I wondered how in the world he'd heard of my class, let alone *why* he'd want to come down to North Bank for a night baking class, but it turns out his firm had purchased pastries from me and he'd liked them so much he looked me up, and that was that."

"So he and Tamera hit it off?"

"You wouldn't believe how terrible of a baker George turned out to be." She laughed just thinking of it. "But, though Tamera has never really baked, she's been around me for years so she stepped in to help. And the rest, they say, is history."

"All right." Adam nodded. "Did he ever mention cases or anything when you were around?"

"You mean did he ever talk about plotting to kill off a star witness? No."

Adam's head jerked up. "How did you know he was a star witness?"

"Simple deduction. But I'm right, aren't I?"

Adam nodded, though he looked like he'd rather be doing anything but. "Last question—for now." He folded his notebook and looked up to meet her gaze. "What do you think about George?"

"Is this off the record?" she asked, indicating his notebook.

"It's more 'next to' the record. I'm asking you for a personal feeling, not fact-based judgment, based on the time you've spent around him."

"I think he's a good guy. I mean, I don't know him as well as Tamera, but I *do* know Tamera. If she trusts him, which she does, then I do too."

Adam nodded and reached for his pocket where he pulled out a buzzing phone. "Sorry. I've got to take this. I'll let you get back to your shop." He hesitated as if he wanted to say something else, but then nodded and went toward the door, pressing the button as he went. "Eastwood here."

She watched him go, wondering about what he'd said. She *did* think George was a good guy, it was obvious he loved her friend, but she didn't know much about him. Maybe it was time to change that.

CHAPTER 4

"Shame 'bout that man who was killed last night. You seen Tamera at all, sweetie?"

Margot shook her head, pushing up her reading glasses. "Sorry, Gladys, I'm just trying to finish this article here."

"Oh sure, sure." The older woman, a regular at the senior center, nodded and placed her other hand on top of her cane that rested upright in front of her. "But really, in *our* little town? What's North Bank comin' to? Turning into the big city. A den of evil, if you ask me."

And that was why Margot *didn't* ask. She kept her attention focused on the screen. Her home computer had ended up in the shop the week before when her power had surged and it suddenly wouldn't turn on. Left with her phone, she decided to use the computers at the local library. Unfortunately, Gladys had found her and wanted to chat, disrupting Margot's research into George Wells' online presence and life.

"And to think Phyllis saw him." The older woman shuddered. "Terrifying."

This drew Margot's attention. "What did you say?"

"I said it's terrifying! I wouldn't want to see a murderer, you know."

"No," Margot felt her heart pounding in her chest. "What did you say before that? Who saw him?"

"Why, Phyllis Henderson of course."

Of course! Margot leaned back, her mind whirring with the new information. "Let me guess, you heard it from Anita?"

"Say, you're really turning into some kind of detective." Gladys practically beamed. "I did. She came down to my room to tea yesterday and told me all about it. Poor Phyllis."

Sure, poor Phyllis. Margot had a feeling she had embellished on what she'd seen. Then again, Margot couldn't be sure until she knew what she'd said.

"Can you tell me what Anita said?"

"Sure, dear, though I thought you were looking in that computer of yours?"

Margot ignored the slight and urged the woman on.

"The way Anita tells it, Phyllis was walking Mr. Golden and—"

"Who?"

"Oh." Gladys gave a throaty laugh that would surely get them kicked out. "Mr. Golden, her corgi. He's very sensitive to heat and must go out at night." Margot nodded so the woman would continue. "Anyway, Anita says that Phyllis says that she was walking down Front

Street when a man in a fedora—of all things—walked past her. That's when she looked up and saw George going into the shop. Can you believe it? She saw him *right* before he committed a murder." The woman gave a look of pure disgust.

Margot wanted to remind her that George was innocent until proven guilty, but she had a feeling it wouldn't do any good.

"Did she say anything else?"

"Not that I can recall. You could talk to Phyllis though, I'm sure she'd tell you." She would, and everyone else who even breathed next to her.

"Thanks so much, Gladys. You've been very helpful."

"Sure thing, sweetie," she said, patting her hand. "Oh! There's the bus—my ride—I'll see you around. Don't forget those nice pastries the next time you stop by the senior center."

Margot agreed and watched her leave before turning back to the recent search she'd put in to the database. So Phyllis was the witness *and* she'd seen a man in a fedora? It was all too bizarre to piece together now.

Margot drew her attention back to the screen. She'd done the usual Google search and come up with nothing more than a little-used Twitter account, a Facebook page, and a few articles where George's name was mentioned in conjunction with his firm.

On a whim, she clicked the second page of results. An article at the top caught her attention.

Victor Carow: Is his fate sealed?

She clicked on it. It was just a basic article written in

the *Washington D.C. Post* that talked about Victor Carow's "reign of terror," as they dubbed it. Apparently, he was a well-known drug lord coming out of Baltimore. What seemed to make him special, though, was the fact that he catered to the elite as well as the average street druggie. That, and the fact that there has been no solid evidence about him specifically.

"How is that possible?" she breathed the question to herself.

She was about to click back to try one more search when a soft voice spoke up behind her. "You're interested in this too, eh?"

Margot looked up to see Wilhelmina leaning down. She blushed and stood up. "I'm sorry, Margot, that was rude." She pushed up her wire-rimmed glasses and tugged at the hem of her royal blue sweater.

"It's all right. What do you mean by 'too'?" Margot leaned forward, wondering what the young librarian could know about Victor Carow.

"Oh, just that Barbara and I were talking about it all this morning." She rubbed her hands up and down her arms as if caught by a chill. "We saw the news this morning that said the star witness in this case had been killed." She indicated the article still up on the screen. "Frightening thinking of *another* murder taking place here in North Bank."

"Yes, very, but what do you mean by 'too'?" Margot felt like a broken record, but she had a vested interest in this. She had promised Tamera she would help George and this information could be valuable. It could also lead nowhere.

"A few weeks back, maybe a month or more, someone came in and was researching that very same thing. I wouldn't have remembered it at all, I actually didn't see the man, but Barbara helped him with the computer—some kind of error code had come up—and she saw that he'd been reading about Victor Carow. I guess Barbara knows someone living in D.C. who's talked about this man and—"

"Sorry, but you don't know who it was?"

"No, dear, Barbara helped him."

"Is Barbara here? I'd like to talk with her."

"Oh, I'm sorry to say she left for her vacation after her shift was over at two."

Margot's hopes fell. "Do you have her phone number?"

"I do," Wilhelmina said but bit her lip, cuing Margot to the fact that she was either nervous about giving it over or something else was wrong.

"I understand you may not want to give it to me, but —" But what? She was trying to get her friend's husband out of jail? That sounded a little too drastic. No need to frighten the poor woman any more than she already was.

"Oh, it's not that," Wilhelmina said with a short laugh. "I just don't think it'll do you any good."

"It won't?"

"Nope. She's gone hiking in the Blue Mountains. She told me she'd be out of service for several days."

Margot contained her groan for the most part. "Can I

get it anyway? Maybe I'll try her now and see if I've caught her before she's out of range."

"Sure thing. I'll be right back," Wilhelmina said, spinning on her ballet flats.

Once Margot had the number, she pressed dial the minute she stepped out of the library but it immediately went to voicemail. Terrific. The first lead she had and there was no way to verify it.

MARGOT BIT her lip as she maneuvered her car down the narrow streets in the older part of town. She had a feeling that Tamera could use some companionship right now and, if she *was* home and not at the police station, Margot was going to console her in any way she could.

Turning down the cobblestone street, she spotted Tamera's light blue car parked in front of her stone row home. George's larger SUV was also parked in front, letting Margot know that Tamera was indeed home, unless she'd gotten a ride to the station.

Taking a chance, Margot parked down the street where a spot was available and walked the block back to Tamera's bright red door. She knocked, but there was no reply. Knocking again, she heard nails on the floor and one bark. So Mr. Puggles was in the house—that probably meant Tamera was too.

"Tam, it's me," she said through the door.

Finally, the door swung open and a furry ball of energy butted up against her legs. "Hello, Mr. Puggles," she said, leaning down to scratch the pug behind the ears. When she stood, she met her friend's gaze. "I couldn't stay away...from Mr. Puggles."

Tamera cracked what almost could have passed for a smile and stepped inside. "You might as well come in. Tea?"

"I'd love some."

They walked into the French country-inspired kitchen painted in bright yellows with deep red accents, figures and pictures of chickens scattered throughout.

"How are you, Tam?" she asked as she slid into a chair at the bar.

"How do you think?" Tamera's back was to Margot, but her inflection was clear. She was on the verge of tears.

"Not good, I'm sure. Do you want me to take you down to the station?"

Setting the kettle on the stove, she turned to face Margot. "Not yet. George said it would take them a while to p-process him." She covered her trembling lips with a hand.

"He's right. But you should go down in a little while. I'll go with you. We can see if Adam will let you talk with George."

Tamera nodded, not trusting herself to speak.

"I know it seems impossible, but think of it this way— the police are only doing their job following up on a lead. They have to take all tips seriously until they find out who did this."

"I know. It's just..." She took a deep breath. "What *was* he doing back so early?"

"What do you mean?" Margot leaned forward, trying to understand what her friend was talking about.

"When they took George into custody, I called his boss —I didn't know what else to do. He assured me that, should he need it, they'll send someone to represent him. He said he'd never seen a harder worker than George. I agreed and said only a man like George would cut his honeymoon short for work."

Margot swallowed. She didn't like where this was going. "It wasn't for work?"

"No." Tears swelled into Tamera's eyes. "He said that he hadn't been called back."

Though Margot was not willing to entertain the idea that her best friend's husband had in fact had anything to do with the murder, the circumstances were starting to become rather suspicious.

Just then the teakettle sang, drawing Tamera away for a moment as Margot considered this new information. If George hadn't come back for work, then why had he come back? There were a million reasons, but it had to be something very strong in order to draw him away from his honeymoon.

Tamera set down a cup of tea in front of Margot and the minty aroma swirled up to greet her. She breathed in and allowed it to calm and refresh her. They would figure this out.

"Marg, do you think—" Tamera couldn't even get the words out.

"No. He didn't do this."

"But—"

"I know it looks…concerning, but we'll get to the bottom of this. The police may have already figured out why he came back."

"I just don't even want to think about the fact that he lied to me, Marg. Lied to my face about having to come back for work. Why would he do that unless…?"

"Tamera," Margot said, waiting until her friend's eyes met hers. "Do you love George?"

"Absolutely."

"Does he love you?"

Tamera took a deep breath and, meeting Margot's gaze, she nodded. "I have no doubt that he does."

"Then that settles it. There's an explanation for everything and we *will* come to the bottom of it. Now let's finish our tea and go to the police station."

CHAPTER 5

MARGOT WALKED next to Tamera as they ascended the steps of the small police station. North Bank, not a large town, wasn't known for its crime, though recent history would tend to disagree with that reality. They stepped into the station, which smelled like stale coffee and sandwiches.

After checking in, they waited only a moment until Adam came into the front room.

"Hello, ladies," he said, looking appropriately grim. The greying hair at his temples gave him a sage look, but Margot could already see that a late night had affected him. His shoulders drooped with the weight of tiredness. "I suppose you're here to see George?"

His question was directed at Tamera and, after looking to Margot, she agreed. "Yes. If I may?"

"I think we can arrange that. Harver," he called into the room, "a moment."

A younger deputy came toward them, his belt cinched up tight to accommodate his lithe frame. "Yes, Detective?"

"Will you escort Mrs. Wells to the holding cell area? Give her some time with her husband, all right?"

"Sure thing, sir." The young man turned to Tamera. "This way, ma'am."

She looked to Margot as if she couldn't bear to go alone, but Margot encouraged her with a slight nod. The pair disappeared into the depths of the building and Margot turned to look at Adam. "Can we talk?"

"Of course." He led the way back to his office and Margot sank into a chair facing his desk.

"Adam, this is ridiculous."

"I assume you're not talking about the fact that I still have my cup of coffee from five a.m. half-full on my desk?"

His attempt at humor warmed her, though it didn't distract from the reality of the station or the fact that she was, once again, back in Detective Adam Eastwood's office. And not to drop off a box of cookies.

"Not exactly."

He propped his elbows on the desk, resting his head in his hands as if it was too tiresome to keep his head upright by itself. "Then you must be talking about George."

She gave him a look that said, *Of course that's what I'm talking about.*

"Look, I know you're friends with Tamera and all, but—"

"It's not just about that. I mean, it is in a way, but—"
She huffed out a breath. "George is no murderer."

"There are a lot of things unknown about the case at
this present moment."

"You sound like a press release," she said, leaning back
and crossing her arms.

"What can I tell you? We still don't have cause of death
from the M.E. yet, we don't know how in the world Mark
Jennings got to North Bank *or* how he got *inside* of
Tamera's shop. Neither do we know the status of George
Wells. It's just..." Adam sighed and roughed a hand over
his face. "Never mind."

"It's just *what* exactly?" She leaned forward.

"How well do you know George Wells?"

Margot felt—as much as saw—the switch in Adam. He
went from tired friend to alert investigator.

"What do you mean? I told you everything this
morning."

"I mean, you are close friends with Tamera. You
introduced her to George, in a manner of speaking."

"I'd hardly say placing them as partners in a cooking
class constitutes introduced. I didn't know much about
him before the start of the class anyway. But I suppose I
did facilitate their relationship in a way."

"Exactly. So tell me more about George? What was he
like in class? What did you know from him before, during,
and after?"

"Why does it feel like I'm being interrogated? Didn't
we go over this earlier?"

"Margot..." He gave her a stern look.

She tossed up her hands. "I knew next to nothing before the class, just that he was going to be coming from Washington, D.C. and said he was happy the class was later so he could avoid traffic."

"Then during the class?"

"It was more than a year ago."

"Think back. You have an exceptional memory."

She leaned back, staring up at the ceiling in thought. "I always have us do introductions. Just fun things. If I remember correctly, he said he was from D.C., a lawyer, and widowed."

"Interesting."

"What? Why is that interesting?"

"It's not much. Most people share something else, right?"

"Not exactly." She thought back to the class. "Tamera shared even less."

"What was your take on him? In the class specifically."

Margot didn't like the way Adam was all but interrogating her, but she reminded herself he was merely doing his job.

"Honestly? I thought he was a good guy. A guy I would be happy to see my friend date—should he ask."

"And what made you think that would be a possibility."

"Chemistry," she said, smirking, "and not just with regards to the baking."

He rolled his eyes and dropped his hands, leaning back in the chair. Inquisitive Adam was gone for the moment.

"I trust him, Adam. You've got the wrong man for this."

"That's just it. I don't trust him. He's hiding—" Adam cut off, his eyes flicking to her.

He swallowed and shook his head, returning his gaze to the ceiling even as his pointer finger tapped lightly on a file on his desk. "Just trust me when I say there are *things* you may not know about the man." His finger pounded the folder one more time.

Margot's thoughts flew to what Tamera had admitted. Was she bound to tell Adam that George hadn't come back for work? Opening her mouth to say something, she was interrupted by Adam's phone.

"Sorry," he said, standing. "I'll only be a minute."

He stepped from the room, closing the door behind him, and she slumped back into her chair. She should tell Adam, he needed to know everything, but they hadn't even proven that George hadn't come back for a good reason. Maybe to surprise Tamera? Though it seemed counterintuitive to leave one's honeymoon to surprise the one you left.

Something about Adam's tapping drew her focus to the file folder on his desk. It had a label from the computer forensics team across the top. Standing, she extended one finger and popped the top of the folder over.

Her heart beat more soundly in her chest as she read upside down. It looked like a printout of an email. Frowning, she scanned the address. It had George's name at the top but the "sent to" line seemed like a made up email address: beaky123@smail.com.

She skipped down to the body of the email. The first line simply read: *It's time.*

She was about to walk around the desk to more easily read the rest of the email when she heard footsteps coming back down the hall. Flicking the file closed, she resumed her seat and tried to act interested in her phone as Adam stepped back inside.

"Sorry about that."

"It's all right," she said, slipping the phone into her bag. "I really should be going. I assume Tamera is about out of time anyway."

He nodded, his shoulders drooping again. "I'm really sorry about this, Margie. You know that I'll do my very best to figure out what's going on here, no matter what, right?"

She stood, nodding and reminding herself to keep her gaze from slipping to the file folder. "I know that, Adam. You're just doing your job." *And I'm doing mine—helping a friend.*

Her thoughts buzzed with the email as she walked down the hall. It was only when she and Tamera were back in the car and heading back to Tamera's house that she realized she hadn't told Adam about George coming back early.

"How was your conversation with George?"

They were almost back to Tamera's house and her

45

friend had been quiet for so long, she'd wondered if she'd fallen asleep after the rush of adrenaline had left her.

Tamera let out a huge sigh just as Margot pulled into a parking space.

"That man," she said, though her tone wasn't angry or as devastated anymore.

"What? What did he say? What happened?"

She hefted another sigh and turned to look at Margot. "He says that he went to the shop to get glue."

Margot frowned. "Glue? What?"

"I know." Tamera shook her head. "He said he was making me something, trying to be 'crafty' like me, and that the one thing he was missing was a glue stick. He says he knew I had a whole stack at the shop so he went there, opened the door, took a glue stick, and left. That's it."

Margot leaned back in her seat, contemplating this. Walmart was closer to Tamera's house, so why would George make the trek down to the shop? Unless he either needed to be there for something else or was in the area.

It would make sense why he hadn't found the body—assuming he was there during the time that Mark was killed or after the fact. But did that mean he'd been close to the killer? Interrupted them perhaps? But no, George would have seen something—unless he hadn't relayed that part to the police or his wife. Margot felt sick to her stomach.

"Did he turn on the lights?"

Tamera pulled her attention from the window. "What?"

"The lights. Did he turn them on when he went in there?"

"I don't know—wait, no. He said he used the flashlight on his phone. He went in the front instead of the back."

"Like we did."

"Yes."

She sat back in her seat, forcing herself not to jump to conclusions. "Where's the glue now?"

"That's just it." Tamera turned weighted eyes toward Margot. "He told the police this—of course, because he wanted to exonerate himself—but they can't confirm that he actually took the glue *and* they can't find it."

Margot frowned. "Where did he say it was?"

"That's just it. He can't remember either."

"I'm confused..." Margot was beginning to doubt this whole story. He was a trial lawyer, he wouldn't just misplace a glue stick. Had George fabricated all of this to get out of telling the truth? Then again, wouldn't he come up with a better story?

But no, she couldn't think like that. He was innocent until proven guilty—which, hopefully, he wouldn't be.

"What he says happened is that he went in, got the glue, then came back to the house. He'd left Mr. Puggles inside and apparently that silly dog had chewed up one of his favorite pairs of slippers while he was out. I think he was mad that we left him with Abby for the two weeks we were gone." Tamera shrugged but continued. "So he had to clean up that whole mess and by the time he was done, I called him and he went right back down to the shop where the rest of this all takes place."

Margot began to nod. "And the slipper?"

"The—what?"

"Is it in the back trash?"

"Yes, I saw it there yesterday."

So one part of his story could be verified. "So then we have to find the missing glue stick—a brand new one—to corroborate his story."

"Yes. As soon as I get home I'm going to tear the house apart looking for it."

"But...why a glue stick? What was he doing?"

She blushed and looked down. "He made me a card. Said he'd looked up tutorials online and wanted to have it done by the time I got back."

Again, it seemed to fit. "Do you have the card?"

"He told me not to look at it yet—even in jail, he's still playing the romantic—but he told me where it is."

"I'll need to look at it."

Tamera nodded. "Margot, I know it sounds farfetched. But with Mrs. Henderson seeing him go into the shop and then the body being found...it just looks bad. But it's all circumstantial—so George says."

It was, but the email Adam had apparently found made it more than that...but she couldn't divulge that information to her friend. At least not yet.

"Well, let's go look."

"What?"

She reached over and grabbed her friend's hand, squeezing lightly. "We'll look for the glue stick and maybe come across something else that will help too."

"I won't give up," Tamera said. "You remember all

those years that I complained to you about being single. All those terrible first dates I went on. All the tears I cried." She rested her head back against the headrest. "It all faded when I met George. He's not perfect and sometimes he drives me nuts—as I'm sure I do to him too—but he's the one, Marg. He's the one meant for me. The one that completes me. I just can't— I can't imagine him doing anything like this. Besides, it makes no sense."

"I know. None of it makes sense."

"No, I mean, why in the world would George kill Mark? *That* makes no sense."

"Because he was a witness?"

"No, because he was *the* witness. I remember the day George came home saying they had finally found someone to testify. It was nothing short of a miracle. George believes in ending what Victor Carow does. He wouldn't jeopardize the trial like that."

Margot nodded and they went into Tamera's house to look for the elusive glue stick, but her thoughts stayed with Victor Carow and the now-dead star witness in the case against him. Was it possible that the emails George had gotten were from him—or someone associated with him?

Had George's loyalty been bought?

CHAPTER 6

THE FEELING of stiff dough beneath her hands made Margot pull back, blinking. She'd gotten lost in thought again and had almost overworked her dough. That was happening more and more. The puzzle of the murder of Mark Jennings was too mind-bending for her to let go. Though, calling it merely a puzzle seemed to lessen what it really was. A murder of a man who had just stepped up to do the right thing.

The front door opened and, looking through her view window, she saw a young man step into the light streaming in from the front window. He had short-cropped blonde hair and a medium build that reminded her of a runner. He looked athletic, but not a gym junkie.

She took all of this in in the moment it took for him to come to the counter and lean down to look through the pass-through.

"Hello." His voice was smooth, probably a tenor if he

sang, and he offered her a kind smile. Not over the top or egotistical, but decidedly confident.

Dusting off her hands, she came through the door and stood behind the counter. "How can I help you?" She didn't ask if he wanted a pastry because she had a sense he wasn't here for that.

"I heard that you had an opening for an assistant. I wanted to apply for the job."

"An—an assistant?" Margot wracked her brain. How had this young man heard that? She hadn't fully admitted to herself that she was interested in hiring, let alone placed an ad anywhere.

"I have a certificate from The Art of Pastry program associated with Kingston College in Vermont. I am a hard worker, and my specialty was in French pastry making. I think I would be a valuable asset to your business."

She blinked. For being so young, she'd guess somewhere in his early twenties, he carried himself well and put forth a compelling argument for hiring him. But there was the matter of him having information she hadn't given to anyone. Well, almost anyone…

"Adam," she said, shaking her head.

The young man tried to hide his grin. "My name is Dexter. Dexter Ross."

"But you know Adam Eastwood, don't you?"

He looked back at her, good-natured guilt written on his features. "I'm originally from New York and knew Adam when I was younger."

"And now you're in North Bank, Virginia. Why is that?"

"I needed a change of scenery."

"And you know French pastry making?"

He nodded vigorously.

"And you have references to go along with this resume I'm assuming you have ready for me?"

He gave her a wicked grin. "Does that mean I can interview for the job?"

She dropped her arms to her side just as Bentley walked in. "Morning, Mar— Who are you?"

The older man eyed Dexter as if he might be able to gain the answer to his question without the boy saying anything.

"I'm Dexter, Mrs. Durand's new assistant." He turned back and winked at her.

He was shameless.

"Meet Dexter," Margot said, trying to hold in her smile, "he's hoping he's lucky enough to prove to me he's up to par to be my assistant."

Bentley eyed him again, giving him a once-over, then he nodded. "One misstep, boy, and she'll take you out." Dexter's eyes widened. "She doesn't take those Krav Maga classes for nothing." Then Bentley turned to Margot. "The usual, dear, if you will."

She smiled at the older man, loving his protective nature. "I'll get that for you in just a moment. Dexter, this way please."

The young man followed her back to the kitchen. "Nice setup you have here."

"Nice setup is exactly what I'd call this." She faced him, arms over her chest.

"Hey," he said, raising his hands up in a defensive position, "Adam only mentioned that there might be a position open here. He said the rest was up to me."

"To charm your way in, huh?" She cracked a smile.

"Does that mean I'm charming?" He grinned again. It was infectious. "He may have mentioned that you don't have much help and are looking for someone who can take some of the burden of baking, not just running the shop. I have expertise in both." Then he reached into the leather satchel that was slung over his shoulder and pulled out a manila folder. "My credentials, references, and competition stats."

She scanned through the work list and had to admit it was impressive. "Chef Corbett? Really?"

He nodded.

"I'll need to follow up on some of this—"

"I expected as much," he said with a congenial smile.

"Why don't I give you a call once I've made my decision."

He inclined his head. "My number is listed at the top. I look forward to hearing from you."

"All right. Thank you, Dexter."

He flashed another confident smile then disappeared through the kitchen door. She heard him say good-bye to Bentley and then was gone. Her hands worked to cut the caramel pecan cinnamon roll for Bentley, but her mind was on the young man. If what she'd read was accurate and not a fabrication, he was more than qualified to work for her. But could she trust him?

Once the order was delivered, she went back into the kitchen and pulled out her phone.

Adam answered on the second ring. "What's up, Margie?"

He sounded distracted but she pressed on. "Do you know a Dexter—" She looked down at the sheet in front of her. "—Ross?"

"Oh Dex," Adam chuckled and then said something muffled before coming back to their conversation. "He's a good kid. You really ought to give him a chance."

"So then his credentials are legitimate."

"Yep." Someone spoke on the other side of the phone. "Are you sure about that?"

"What?" Margot asked.

"Right, we'll get it up here however you need to. I need a look inside ASAP."

"Adam?" she tried again, knowing that he wasn't speaking to her now.

"Sorry," he said, coming back to their conversation. "We think we just found the car that Mark drove down to North Bank."

MARGOT PICKED up her pace as she walked from where she'd parked at the small turn out down Route 1. Adam stood with his back to the sun, squinting as a large tow truck with a winch attached to the back worked at pulling up the car over the side of the ridge.

"Margot, what are you doing here?"

She skirted a few officers who were taking pictures and writing notes. "You said you found the car."

He frowned at her. "Did you think that was an invitation to come down here?"

"Wasn't it?"

He laughed. "No, but since you're here." He indicated the cliff face. "Take a look."

She walked with him to the side and they looked over the edge. The sheer rock wall dove to the river at an impressive angle that only began to lesson twenty feet from the water. It was there that the car had landed, front end down. She also saw a worker rapelling down the cliff face toward the car. Even from this height they could see that the back license plate had been marred by something —was that paint?

"Do you think the murderer took pains to paint the license plate?"

"It would seem that way."

"But George—"

"I know. We're following up on all of this." She pressed her lips together and he looked down at her. "Hey, I don't want it to be George just as much as you do, but unfortunately there is still time in the timeline for him to, conceivably, have done this."

"How is that even possible?" she asked, looking around. "The killer had to have come here, set the car to drive off the cliff, and then *somehow* made it back to civilization on foot."

"Margie," he said, a pained look coming onto his

handsome features. "We're not that far from where Tam and George live."

She blinked, looking around again. What Adam said was true. Though this area of the road was faced by sheer cliffs, there was a popular beach not more than a mile or so down the road from there. Because of that, there were many paths that led from the small communities to the river access. She could pick out the exact path that would lead to Tamera and George's street from where she stood.

This was not good.

"Still—"

"I'm not ruling anything out."

"Hey, Detective Eastwood," a man called out to him.

"Yeah, Hal, what is it?"

Margot walked over with him, not interfering but still wanting to know what the man had to say.

"Looks like my guy has a solid lock on the car."

Margot swallowed. Hopefully the worker would return to the safety of this side of the cliff soon.

"Great. Can you start pulling it up?"

The man nodded. "Yep. Wanted to get your OK first."

"You have it."

The man nodded and turned back toward his team. "Haul her up!"

A terrible scraping sound ensued as the winch worked overtime to pull the heavy car up from the cliff. Margot kept her arms wrapped around her, the wind coming from the river chillier than normal despite the warm, humid day.

"You really should hire him," Adam said out of the

blue. They had been standing, mesmerized by the slow process to bring the car up, when he broke into her thoughts.

"What?"

"Dex. He's a good kid. A little too creative at times," he said, smirking to himself, "but a good kid. I'll vouch for him."

"So he's as talented as his resume says he is."

"More than," Adam said. Something in the way he said it caused her to file that piece of information away for later.

"I have to admit that it's tempting. He's got a good resume and, once I see how he does in the kitchen, I could use a break every now and again. It'll be slow going though—to make sure he's up for it."

"He will be."

She shook her head and her silence drew his attention. "What?"

"You're impossible."

"Hey," he said, turning to face her, his hands sliding onto his hips, "I see how hard you work. I know you're there every morning before the sun is even up. You barely have any time for yourself. In fact, I actually saw you more when Taylor was here than I have in the past few years—and that was just for a few months."

She smiled at the memory of her niece and the great help she'd turned out to be. But her smile faded at the look in Adam's eyes. Why was this so important to him?

"It's just the life of a baker—"

"No, it's not. You work harder than anyone I know and

I think you deserve to take a break every now and again." He shrugged. "Maybe go out to dinner. With me."

Suddenly the shift in the wind wasn't the only thing that had changed. This conversation had gone from banter to seriousness within the span of a moment.

"We've had dinner lots of times," she said, trying to defend her tendency to overwork.

"I'm not talking about me bringing you Chinese at the bakery because I know you haven't eaten. I'm talking about...dinner." He cleared his throat and his eyes skipped to the men still working to bring up the car. "Like, a dinner date."

Margot felt everything slow down for a moment. Was Detective Adam Eastwood asking her on a date? She opened her mouth then closed it, unsure if she knew what to say or not. The look in his eye pleaded with her to say something, and she knew he deserved that much, but she was struck utterly speechless.

"Margot, I—" he began but a shout from the crew drew their attention.

"The car is up," she said, too much relief sinking into her words.

They rushed to the car and the first thing Adam did was check the front license plate.

"Collier, take down this plate number. I want you to run it ASAP."

"Yes, sir," the young deputy said, rushing to his side. Once he had it, he ran off to his squad car with the plate number and Adam stood by as one of the workers pried open the passenger side door. When it stood wide open, though leaning toward the ground unnaturally, Adam ducked inside to the glove box.

Margot couldn't help her curiosity and slipped up next to him to peer over his shoulder. She may have been somewhat blindsided by his request but her attention was back on the case as she knew his was.

"Is that the registration card?"

"Yes, and it looks like the car is registered to…" He squinted. "A Christina Jordan. It's a D.C. address."

"But, Adam, who is Christina Jordan?"

He looked down at her, tapping the paper against the mangled roof of the car. "I don't know, but I aim to find out."

CHAPTER 7

I~T HAD TAKEN~ all of her convincing and a sheer bit of luck, she was sure, but Margot had convinced Adam to let her come along to D.C. while they questioned Christina. Thankfully, he hadn't brought up his mention of dinner again.

Part of Margot knew she wanted to say yes to him. What she'd said was true, they had had dinner on multiple occasions, but what he was asking was *more* than dinner and she still wasn't sure she was ready for that. Besides, if the current situation was any indication, they would be busy for quite some time solving this case.

Correction. Adam would be busy solving the case. She would merely be busy keeping George out of jail.

They took the 4th Street exit into Washington, D.C. and Adam maneuvered them through the light day traffic. She was surprised, expecting it to be more congested, but it was still early. They turned up Independence Avenue and Margot saw the Capitol building, the dome shining and bright after its recent construction. The tall House and Senate buildings gave way to the Library of Congress and the Jefferson Building.

Paused at a stoplight, Adam turned to look at her. "I shouldn't have let you come with me."

"Oh, Adam," she said, giving him a look that said he was being foolish. "You called and talked with this woman. She's a librarian at Georgetown. How dangerous can this be?"

He smirked and shook his head. "You do have a point there. Though something's been bothering me."

"What's that?"

"According to his file, Mark lives down the street from Christina."

"And?"

"Well, the dates are funny to me. As is the fact that she —a librarian at Georgetown as you've so nicely pointed out—lives in Capital Hill."

Margot followed his logic. "When did she move in?"

"January."

"And Mark—"

"Moved in last June, right before the trial."

"You think she could be involved in all of this? Really? A librarian?"

He smirked. "I'm not in the business of making guesses. Librarian or not, she could be dangerous. She could be a plant from Victor's gang. I should have done more research before coming." He said the last part to himself, but Margot reached over and rested her hand on his arm.

"I know how to take care of myself."

"But you shouldn't have to—not if I've done my job well."

They were maneuvering through the one-way streets, Adam checking each street sign until he saw 7th Street. Taking a left, he went two and a half blocks then he pulled into a spot in front of a white and green row house. Turning off the car, he paused and looked toward Margot.

"I want you to pay attention and stay behind me."

"What's she going to do? Come at us with the Dewey Decimal System?" He didn't seem to appreciate her humor. "I will. I promise."

Apparently satisfied with her answer, he got out of the car. She followed as they took the steep steps up to the black front door, a cheery 4th of July-inspired wreath still hanging from a hook. Adam pressed the doorbell and they waited.

When the door opened, the woman in front of them looked so unlike any librarian Margot had ever seen. She wore black skinny jeans, a long black t-shirt that read *"Cats & Coffee"* in bold white lettering, and had dyed black hair cropped at her jawline.

"Uh, Miss Jordan?"

"Nah, that's my roommate. Chrissy!" the girl yelled into the house. "You've got company." She stepped back, an expression of sheer indifference on her face. "You can come in."

"Thank you," Adam said.

They stepped inside into a wide-open space that held an eclectic mix of styles. From a winged back chair by the faux fireplace to a Papasan chair pushed into a corner near a toppling pile of books. The artwork was equally as mismatched. As if the classical style had met impressionism but, like water and oil, didn't mix.

The sound of someone in heels descending the stairs drew their attention toward the narrow staircase. First appeared kitten heels on tiny feet, then a narrow, black pencil skirt, followed by a floral print blouse, necklace of pearls, and then a softly smiling face. The tiny, dark rimmed glasses perching on the nose of the woman before them completed the look. It was classic librarian, except...

Margot jerked her eyes up when she realized she was staring, but the woman in front of her had all manner of tattoos on both arms peeking out just below the forearm-length blouse she wore. Was that indication of a gang affiliation? Or just an affinity for decorative skin ink?

"Hello, can I help you?"

"Miss Jordan, I'm detective Adam Eastwood. We spoke on the phone earlier."

"Oh yes, please, have a seat." She indicated the winged back chair and small love seat. Margot took the chair, Adam the love seat, and Christina pulled over the footstool to the Papasan chair.

"I assume you've heard in the news..." Adam hesitated.

"About Mark? Yeah, I've heard."

Margot watched as she tugged at the edge of her skirt even though it was already over her knee. Was she nervous? But as Margot watched her expression, she saw something else. Sadness.

"You were close with Mark?" Margot asked.

Christina nodded, her lower lip trembling.

"May I ask what the nature of your relationship was?"

Christina met Adam's gaze. "Why?"

"Miss Jordan..." He softened his tone. "Christina. We found your car at the bottom of a cliff. With Mark dead and the car the one connection to how Mark came from D.C. to North Bank, it's imperative we have your full cooperation."

"Look, if I'd known—" Her voice broke, but she swallowed and tried again. "I never would have lent him my car. Never."

"So, you were in a relationship with him?" Margot asked, hoping that gentle reminder would encourage the woman to share more.

"Yeah. No. I mean, I thought we were moving that direction."

She sniffed and Margot handed her the box of tissues from the marble top, claw-footed table next to her chair. One of the tattoos poked out when Christina's sleeve pulled up and Margot caught a glimpse of the shape of a book. Probably *not* gang tattoos then.

"I met Mark at a coffee shop down the street a few years ago. We talked, he liked books, and we hit it off. At the time I was still living in Georgetown, but I liked to take the weekends to explore new parts of D.C. You know, see the sights in my own city."

Margot nodded, encouraging her with a smile.

"Then this whole trial thing happened. We had to stop seeing each other for a while and I really missed him. Like *really* missed him. My lease was up and I'd found out from Mark where they had relocated him so I...moved." She blushed and looked down. "Sounds desperate, right? I really cared for him and hoped we could, you know, make a go of it. Try out a relationship."

"So explain to me why he had your car?"

"My car and my favorite hat," she said with a humorless laugh.

Margot and Adam exchanged glances.

"He said he needed to run a few errands. I let him use my car all the time but he usually was going to the store so he wouldn't need to lug things around. And there was usually someone with him—protection, you know? He kept my keys and when I looked outside the other night, the car was gone. I figured he had to run an errand but got really worried when he didn't show back up. Then I saw the news—" She clutched the tissue to her nose.

"What do you mean he borrowed your hat?"

Christina sniffed loudly. "He said he needed to borrow a fedora. I didn't question it." She let out a long sigh. "I don't know what else I can tell you."

A fedora. The pieces began to fit. The makeup on the inside of the hat now made perfect sense.

Thanking Christina and making sure she had his card in case she thought of anything else, Adam thanked her for her time. Then they left, the sounds of the busy city greeting them and Christiana's words circulating in the air around them.

∾

ADAM PULLED BACK on to 395 and turned the radio down. Margot glanced to the side, trying to read him. She'd been around him enough to know that he needed time to process things. She would be surprised if he brought up the case now, because she had a feeling he needed to mull over what they had heard.

"So, Dex," he began.

She huffed out a breath. "You've got to be kidding."

He grinned at her, his eyes staying on the road. Part of her wondered if he'd bring up going to dinner again, but another part of her hoped he wouldn't. Now *she* was the one who needed processing time.

"He's a good kid," Adam said in a singsong voice.

"I know. I just...I haven't had time to go over his credentials and—"

"What? A recommendation from me isn't good enough? What if I told you I've already run a background check on him?"

"You did?"

"Would that change you hiring him?" He looked hopeful.

"Adam, why are you insistent on me hiring Dexter?"

Adam let out a deep breath. "He told you he knew me, right?"

"Yes, he mentioned he knew you when he was younger."

"Well..." Adam swallowed. Was he uncomfortable? "I actually took care of him for a while. While his mom was...unavailable."

"Unavailable?"

Adam cringed again. "Drugs. She was in rehab."

Margot's whole notion of Adam shifted in that moment. He had long since been her friend and before that he'd been a friend of her husband, Julian's, but now he was more. A guardian. Almost a parent.

"Really." It was a statement more than a question.

He risked a glance at her. "What? What's going on in that sharp mind of yours, Margot Durand? You have me worried."

She smiled. "I'm just picturing you as a...guardian. That's really commendable of you."

"Now don't go putting me on a pedestal. He needed a place to stay and I had a spare bedroom. It was kind of like what you did for Taylor, just a little longer."

"How long?"

He took in a breath. "Two years."

"Two—!" She cut herself off, the exclamation clearly making Adam uncomfortable. Though he was the town's only detective and could take over a case with bravado, Adam was the furthest thing from a man who wanted attention drawn to his good deeds.

"It was the right thing to do."

"I believe that."

Silence rested between them but Margot's mind filled in pictures of Adam as a guardian. It was a pleasant picture.

"So..." He drew the word out. "Dex."

"All right," she laughed, shaking her head, "I'll hire him."

"Yes!" he said, sounding way too excited.

"But on a *trial* basis. He needs to prove himself to me first."

"Naturally. You know, when he was younger—" Adam's story was cut off by his phone. He pressed a button on his steering wheel and the sound crackled through the car speakers. "Eastwood here."

"Well howdy, Detective E," a booming voice said. Margot leaned back, as if to get away from the loudness of the voice, and Adam pressed another button. "It's Martin the M.E." The man laughed on the other end of the line but thankfully his voice was quieter now.

"He says that *every time* he calls me," Adam whispered to Margot. She grinned and pressed her lips together when the man spoke again.

"You got someone there with you?"

"Yes. Mrs. Durand from the bakery."

"Oh, great! I've been meaning to stop by, Margot. Wife's got a birthday coming up and—"

"Did you have something for me, Martin?" Adam interrupted.

"Yup, sure do. But I can call back…" His meaning was clear.

"I think it'll be all right for Margot to hear."

"Sure enough," Martin said. "I've got the tox screen results back on that fellow."

Margot's hopes soared. Would they reveal some way to clear George?

"Go ahead," Adam said.

"Looks like it was a lethal dose of Digoxin."

"Really," Adam said, pondering the results.

"But there was something else."

"Go ahead, Martin."

"Looks like there were trace amounts of insulin in the syringe. We wouldn't have seen it in the blood work but I of course sent off everything we found to The Big Guys."

"He always calls them that," Adam whispered, eliciting another laugh from Margot.

"So the syringe previously had insulin in it. Had it been used before?"

"Nope. My best guess here is that the culprit emptied out a diabetic syringe and filled it with a homemade killing remedy."

"Homemade?" Margot clamped her mouth shut. She hadn't meant to interfere but her curiosity had gotten away from her.

"Yes sir—er, ma'am. Digoxin is found in foxglove."

"Like the flower?"

"The very same."

Adam nodded as if he'd already known this.

"Anything else, Martin?"

"Not yet. I'll call when I know more."

"Thanks."

"Sure thing, boss. Bye, Margot."

He hung up and the car fell into silence again. A diabetic syringe filled with a homemade poison made from flowers found all over George's neighborhood—and even his front yard. Things were looking worse and worse for her friend's husband.

CHAPTER 8

DEXTER WAS WAITING at the door when Margot arrived at the shop early the next day. Startled, she took a step back when he emerged from the shadows.

"Sorry to scare you," he said with an infectious grin. "I just believe in being on time."

"Or early," she said, unlocking the door and typing in her code for the alarm system. "Welcome to your first day at the bakery."

"I'm looking forward to it."

"Just so you know, this is—"

"A trial period," he said, interrupting her, but not rudely. "I know. And I appreciate the chance."

Feeling slightly better about things and the reality that she would have help that morning, she put Dexter to work prepping the kitchen as she sat down behind her desk for the first few sips of coffee before the busyness began. She felt slightly guilty for making him work while she eased into the morning, but then again—that was what assistants were for, right? Besides, she was paying him well, even if it was a trial period.

Checking her email, she clicked on one that was marked from the library. Did she have a book she was late in returning?

When the email opened, she saw it was addressed to her from Barbara at the library. Margot had almost forgotten about talking with Wilhelmina and how Barbara had been gone on vacation.

She skimmed through the short email surprised to see that Barbara had cut her trip short due to a sprained ankle and that she would be at the library—on crutches—if Margot wanted to stop by that afternoon.

Margot wondered if Wilhelmina had told her what her questions regarded, but the scent of something burning drew her attention to the kitchen.

"What is—" She stopped short to see Dexter bent over an amazing creation of spun sugar.

"Sorry about that," he said, standing up after resting the spoon on the counter. "Some of the sugar got onto the element."

"What are you making?"

"I hope you don't mind," he said, looking sheepish, "but when you said you were going to be making mini-cheesecakes, I thought about these spun sugar toppers. They are easy to make and it was something I could get out of the way now. I should have asked," he finished, looking nervous.

She smiled, impressed not only by his talent but his creativity. "I'm impressed. Though I will say you probably should have consulted me before using my ingredients. What if I wouldn't have enough for what we're making next?"

His expression fell. "I should have thought of that."

"It's all right. You did well with these and, thankfully, I'm fully stocked. Let's get to work, shall we? These desserts aren't going to bake themselves."

The rest of the morning flew by, and with Dexter's help, Margot was pleased to see that they were done well ahead of her planned schedule. Stepping back as the last of the cookies were pulled from the oven, she surveyed the kitchen. It was a little messier than when she worked by herself, but finishing nearly an hour earlier, and it only being Dexter's first day, seemed to make her choice to hire him obvious.

Then again, she wasn't going to tell him that just yet. Better to let him sweat it out just a few more days. Besides, the first day could be a fluke. Though she had a feeling it wasn't. He was a hard worker and a talented baker.

The front doorbell rang and Dexter popped his head out, a cheery greeting of hello welcoming guests. He sure was enthusiastic.

"Who on God's green earth are you?"

Margot pressed her lips together to keep her laugh in. Should she go out and rescue Dexter from Rosie's inquisition? Or let him sweat a little?

Deciding he'd already been through enough, she stepped into the front space of her shop. "Rosie, why are you giving my new employee a hard time?"

Rosie's chocolate brown eyes widened, the white stark against her brown skin. "New employee, did you say?"

"Yes. This is his first day." Margot crossed her arms, looking between them.

"He's not replacing me, child." She said it as fact, no question in her statement.

Margot let her laugh float out at the look on Dexter's face. "No, Rosie! Of course not! No one could replace you."

"That's right," she said, placing a hand on her hip. "What's he doing for you then?"

"He," Dexter said, breaking into the conversation, "is going to go clean up the kitchen."

He rushed off before Margot could tell him she'd help, but she turned back to Rosie. "Adam recommended him to me."

"Detective Eastwood?" Rosie perked up at his name. "Well then, in that case."

Margot rolled her eyes. "I could say Adam ran into your car and you'd still get that look on your face."

"He's a fine young man," Rosie said, her grin widening. "And I do mean *fine*."

"Oh, Rosie," she said, shaking her head. The two women gave into laughter just as Margot heard the kitchen sink turn on. "I should probably go back and help him. But what are you doing here early?"

"I came by to ask if I could get in a few extra hours this week. It's my granddaughter's birthday next month and I want to get her something special. A few extra hours would really help."

Margot smiled warmly back at the older woman. "Of course, Rosie. Anything you need. In fact…" She looked back toward the kitchen. "Maybe I'll leave Dexter in your watchful charge."

Rosie burst into a deep-throated laugh. "You know I'll teach him right."

"I do know that," Margot said.

After Margot explained what Dexter needed to do for the rest of his shift, she collected her items and stepped out into the fresh air. The library wasn't far from the bakery and she decided to take advantage of the perfect weather to walk.

When she reached the front door, she smoothed her hand over her hair and stepped inside. The quiet interior boasted only a few occupants, which at this time of day, she wasn't surprised. It was close to lunch and many in the senior community didn't leave their homes until later in the day.

She made her way to the front desk and was happy to find Barbara there. The woman reached for her crutches, but Margot held out a hand.

"Mind if I come to you instead?"

"Please," Barbara said, looking relieved.

They chatted pleasantly at first as Margot asked how Barbara's trip had gone and how recovery for her ankle was going. When there was a lull, Margot edged closer to her real question. She wanted to play it carefully knowing that, in their little retirement community, the library was quite a hub for gossip and Margot didn't want to be the one drawing attention to anything unnecessarily. At least not yet.

"So, Barbara, I was in here talking to Wilhelmina a few days ago."

"Oh, I know, she told me you wanted to see me. It's why I sent you that email last night. Almost forgot to. Had to log on right before I left."

"And I appreciate that." She hesitated. How would she word this? "So, there was a man researching something similar to what I was. At least that's what Wilhelmina said."

"Sure was." Barbara shivered. "Strange—and downright scary if you ask me—that he was looking into a man who ended up dead. Are you looking into the case? I know you solved that murder mystery at the beginning of summer. You going to do the same now? Seems like you've got a head for mystery."

Not the subtlety Margot was hoping for. "Not exactly. I'm just curious about this person. Could you describe him?"

"Well, sure," she said, her gaze traveling up to some distant spot in the ceiling. "He was white, tall, balding, medium build. Kind of average looking. I think he had light brown hair."

Margot groaned. It sounded a lot like George, but she couldn't be sure." Her hand flew to her pocket, but she realized with a grimace that she'd left her phone back at the bakery on her desk so there was no way to show Barbara a recent picture of George.

"He wasn't in here long. Sorry I can't be of more help to your case."

Margot groaned inwardly. "Not *my* case. The police's case." She forced a smile and stood. "Thank you for all you help. Hope your ankle feels better soon."

"Thanks, dear. And good luck. I know you can solve it."

Margot gave the woman a tightlipped smile and left. She wasn't solving anything. Merely looking into leads. Leads that seemed to keep coming back to George.

"I DON'T KNOW, MARG," Tamera said, picking at her pasta halfheartedly. "I think someone is dragging their feet."

Tamera was surprised to learn that George still hadn't had his bail hearing. "Who's the judge?"

"Judge Castor. Something about him being sick and then the courtroom was double-booked. Does that even happen?"

Margot had no idea and merely shrugged, her bite of garlic bread melting in her mouth. "How are *you* doing with him being gone?"

Tamera looked off into the distance. "I don't know. I just keep thinking…"

"Thinking what?"

"That maybe I don't know him as well as I thought I did."

"Tamera..." Margot shook her head and reached across the table to grasp her friend's hand. "That is nonsense. You know him just fine and we both believe in his innocence. It's just a difficult time right now. What George needs is for you to be beside him. Remember the 'in sickness and in health' part of your vows?"

"I don't know if that applies here, Marg," she said, looking doubtful.

"Maybe not," Margot said through a grin, "but I think part of all of that is that it's in good times and in bad. These are the bad. So stick by him."

Tamera's eyes filled with tears. "You're right. Oh, Marg, I'm so sorry. This was awful of me. Of *course* I'm going to stick by him."

"Nonsense. You're being honest with me and I appreciate that. I know it's not easy. We all have our moments, but I know at the end of the day that you love him and will stick up for him."

She nodded and the waiter appeared with their check and to-go boxes. "No Antonio tonight?" Margot asked the young woman.

"No, his sister just came back from Italy so he's spending some time with her," the girl replied with a smile.

"Glad to hear she made it back." Margot paid for the meal and they left, getting into Tamera's car since Margot had left hers at Tamera's house.

"Need anything else before we go back to your place?" Margot asked. "You do have food at home, don't you?"

"Yes, mother," Tamera said with a smile as she pulled out onto the road.

Margot laughed and leaned back. Nighttime had fallen while they'd eaten dinner and now it was dark, dim lights popping up in business, streetlights, and the porch lights of most homes they passed.

As Margot leaned back, bright headlights reflected in the side mirror and she held up a hand to block their penetrating brightness.

"Gosh, this guy is right on my tail," Tamera said, both hands gripping the wheel.

"Does he have his brights on?"

"Seems like it, right?" Tamera took the next turn onto Route 6, a road that ran parallel to Highway 1, and followed along the river. The road was narrow and winding, but for a longtime North Bank resident like Tamera, they were as natural as driving through town every day.

The lights behind them seemed to get brighter. "Wow, he must be in a rush."

"Tell me about it," Tamera said, her jaw clenching with each turn. "I'm pushing five over the speed limit as it is, but he's still getting really close."

Margot turned around in her seat, trying to shield her eyes from the bright light to see if she could catch the make of the car—or perhaps it was a truck?—but it was too bright to tell.

Then Tamera sucked in a breath as they went around a particularly sharp curve and Margot whipped around to the front again.

"Margot!" she said as the sound of the vehicle's revving engine behind them was so close that Margot thought it was vibrating through her seat.

"Be careful, Tam—" Margot said just as they felt the vehicle hit Tamera's car from behind.

Tamera screamed but kept her eyes on the road. Margot reached up to grab the handle above her door to keep from flying forward just as the vehicle behind them struck again.

"I can't keep this up much more, Marg. This guy's going to push me off the road!"

"It's okay, Tam. You've got this. Just keep it steady." Margot's heart was racing but she forced her mind to calm down. They were coming up on one stretch of road with a bridge. Did the person behind them know about it? If he did, then they most certainly needed to make it past the bridge.

"Speed up."

"Are you joking? I'm already going ten miles over the speed limit."

"Do it! If he's at all close to us near Castle Rock Bridge, we could be pushed over the side."

It was all the encouragement Tamera needed. She pushed down on the gas, creating distance between them and the man behind them.

"What about *after* the bridge?"

"You're going to take The Fork."

Margot watched Tamera's face for any sign that she didn't understand, but all she saw there was determination.

"I'm going to have to hit the brake, though."

"Wait until after we're past the bridge. If you keep enough distance, we should make it."

They waited in tense silence as the bridge came into view. As they had expected, the vehicle sped up, trying to get close to them again.

"Margot…" Tamera said through clenched teeth.

"We're almost there. Just hold on…"

Both women fell silent as they passed the entrance to the bridge. Halfway through, the vehicle sped up again but Tamera had anticipated the move and was already accelerating off of the bridge.

Now came the tricky part. She began to slow. The person behind them came up on them quickly but, at the last moment, she yanked the wheel to the side.

Margot had been prepared for the jolt, or so she'd thought, but the sudden change from paved road to gravel threw both of them forward then back as much as Tamera's ample pressure on the brake.

Eventually, they skidded to a stop on the long, graveled road. Both were panting and both had white knuckles.

"I think he's gone."

Margot turned and saw only darkness behind them.

"That was smart thinking, using The Fork."

Margot took in another breath. She and Tammy often hiked in the hills near the Potomac and they had lovingly name this road The Fork after the first time they'd agreed to meet here and Tamera had called Margot several times to verify its location.

"I'll never forget where this road is. Daylight, nighttime, it doesn't matter."

"And that's what I was counting on. Hopefully, they won't take the time to turn around and come back."

"You think they would?" Tamera's voice held a tremor.

"I don't know, but I'm calling Adam."

CHAPTER 9

"MARGOT, ARE YOU ALL RIGHT?" Adam rushed up the hillside, his lights shining up to where Tamera's car had finally come to a stop. Thankfully, the car was no worse for wear, but the women's nerves were frayed. Another officer, a friend of theirs, stepped into the light and made his way toward Tamera.

"I have never been so scared, Adam," Margot admitted. Her arms were wrapped around herself as if she was cold, but it was more to keep from shaking than anything else.

"I'm so sorry— I..." There was nothing for him to say. And there was no way he could have helped prevent the chase. But the question remained: why them?

"I...I just don't understand. Why us?"

Adam's jaw tightened. "I'm not sure either. I've had some news, but—" He looked around the scene. "If Drake takes Tamera back to her place, can I take you home? So we can talk?"

"Of course, but let me make sure Tamera's all right

with that first."

After explaining the situation to Tamera, she agreed and allowed Officer Drake to slip behind the wheel. Having him drive home would be safer than either of them driving the car. Then Adam got behind the wheel and headed off toward Margot's home.

She clasped her hands in her lap, knowing that they would shake and give away how she was truly feeling if she let them rest on her legs. Since they were close to the house, Adam didn't say anything and she instinctively knew that he would wait until they reached the safety and comfort of her home. It was a fact she was thankful for.

At her townhome, he saw her inside and seated on the couch, while he went to make a mug of peppermint tea. Only when they were seated on the couch, facing one another, and Margot had her mug of tea did he start the conversation she knew they had to have.

"What happened?"

She'd appreciated his earlier care for her, but now she felt overwhelmed by the details that she needed to convey to him. She started at the beginning, where she and Tamera had been and where they'd been planning to go—back to Tamera's place to decompress with a funny movie.

Then she described how the vehicle, now she was thinking it was an SUV, had come up quickly on them as if knowing the right time to approach.

"But wait," he said, interrupting her, "you said a few miles past when you turned onto Route 6 that the guy got close to you."

"Yes," she said, uncertain of why he sounded confused.

"But you also said that he knew the right time to sneak up on you."

"Yes, I could clearly tell that he was waiting for Castle Rock Bridge."

"Right." The lines on Adam's forehead deepened.

"What? I don't understand your confusion."

"I don't know if this guy—assuming it's a guy—knew about Castle Rock Bridge or not, but I do know that he had ample opportunities to run you off the road before that. I also know that he could have circled back to follow you up The Fork if he'd wanted to, but he didn't."

She reasoned through what Adam had said and then nodded in agreement. "I suppose I could be too close to the situation. I assumed he knew about the bridge, but maybe he didn't. Where does that leave us?"

"It leaves us with someone who may not be from the area."

Margot leaned back, her mug of tea reaching a drinkable temperature. She took a sip, contemplating what Adam was saying.

"What do you know that I don't?"

His head jerked up and he met her gaze. "How do you do that?"

"What?"

"Know when I have information that you don't have." A corner of his mouth tipped up.

"Well...?" She waited, knowing he would tell her.

"I've been going over George's bank records."

Margot was suddenly suspicious. "What did you find?"

"I'm not sure, and it's *not* conclusive, but I have reason to believe that George was being blackmailed."

Margot felt her eyebrows rise. "By who?"

"No way to know."

"So…we're talking about cash then."

He nodded, obviously impressed.

"And I would assume similar, large withdrawals at a specific time interval."

"Yes and no. Over the past number of years, significant withdrawals of cash have been made, like you're saying, but they aren't at regular intervals, which is why it took our tech a while to pinpoint. They seem random."

"So maybe as needed?"

"It appears that way."

Margot put together what she knew of George and what she'd learned so far. He was a well-off lawyer in D.C. so he wouldn't be hurting for money. Tamera's business was not only successful in town and to upper class D.C. residents who liked to 'get out of the city,' but also online where she sold supplies on Etsy.

If she had to guess, she assumed they hadn't yet incorporated their finances since they'd only been married a few months. George could have easily hidden blackmail payments he was making if they weren't large enough to wipe him out.

"But, what's more—and possibly what's worse," Adam said, drawing her attention back from her thoughts, "is the fact that he made the largest withdrawal he's made right after he got back to North Bank from Hawaii."

"Oh, Adam…" Margot's mind raced back to the night

when she'd spoken with Tammy. His eyes snapped to hers.

"What?"

"I'm so sorry, I meant to tell you this but forgot. Tammy says that she called his work and he didn't need to come back from his honeymoon for a work event."

"I already know." He looked pained. "And that's not even the worst of it. He deposited the *same* amount of money the night we found Mark."

Margot's eyes widened. "What?"

"It's not looking good for your friend."

"But it doesn't add up."

"Murder usually doesn't."

"No." Margot set her tea down because she felt the need to talk with her hands. "I mean think of it this way— George is *paying* someone for all these years and then what? Suddenly decides to kill a star witness who seems to have no connection to George aside from George's company's involvement in his case? It makes no sense."

"Or George takes a payment to kill off the witness to replace the money he owes his blackmailer. A trade."

Stumped, Margot slumped back against the couch. It still didn't add up for her.

"It's late, and I should go, but I just wanted to make sure you were all right. I don't know who was after you ladies tonight, but I'll get to the bottom of this." He rested a warm hand on her shoulder. "And I want you to be careful. Promise me you will."

"Of course. I'm always careful."

"Careful to get into trouble." He gave her a rueful

smile. "But seriously, Margie, I told you these things in confidence, not so that you'll do something foolish like take this case on by yourself."

She made a mental note of the fact that he hadn't forbidden her from the case, just taking it on by herself. Likely he'd just misspoken, but she'd hold him to it.

"I understand."

They stood and she walked him to the door. When he paused to look at her, she saw compassion in his eyes. His hand on her shoulder was warm as he leaned down and kissed her on the forehead. It was a sweet, caring thing and it helped ease the tension in her body from that night's frightening ride.

"Good night, Adam. And thank you for coming to my rescue…again."

He grinned. "Always."

MARGOT GRIMACED as her alarm shattered the silence of her room. It was still dark out, it always was when she got up for work, but after the car chase the night before, she hadn't been able to fall asleep as easily as she'd wanted. Tossing and turning most of the night, she felt like the car had hit her and Tamera instead of almost forcing them off the road.

Still, she showered, dressed, and made it to the bakery on time as usual. Dexter was there waiting for her and they got right to work. She questioned him on how things had gone after she left the day before and he gave her a rundown of what he'd done.

She was impressed at his skill not only in baking but also in the business side of things. He'd drafted a few proposals for her to look at regarding her website, current marketing she did, and improvements for special events she could host.

"Are you trying to take over my bakery?" she asked.

His hands stilled, one holding a wooden spoon and the other a metal bowl. "N-no," he said, eyes wide.

She broke in to a grin. "Don't worry, Dex," she said, using the nickname Adam used for him, "I'm just joking with you."

He let out a huge sigh. "You got me."

"But, in all seriousness, I really appreciate your proactive approach to working here. You're a good baker, but you also have great business sense."

"Thank you."

"Now let me ask you this," she said, leveling her gaze at him so he'd know she was serious. "Why are you really here?"

Was it her imagination or had he paled at her question?

"Uh, what do you mean?"

"I've checked into your credentials. Not only are you certified, but you've also got a bachelor's degree in business and you're just shy a few credits of having your master's in business management. I've called a few of your past references and they've loved working with you. Some even expressed regret over you leaving, as if they'd lost a vital part of their business." She placed her hands on the cool, stainless steel countertop and leaned forward. "Don't get me wrong, I'm happy you're here, but I don't want to start relying on you only to have you split a few months later. I think knowing why you're really here will help me decide whether or not I'll keep you on."

He blinked a few times in the silence that fell between them but then he slowly began nodding. He wiped his flour-caked hands on his apron and crossed his arms. His demeanor was in no way closed, just thoughtful.

"You're a smart woman, Mrs. Durand. Though Adam already warned me of that."

"He did, did he?"

"Yep." He grinned but then continued, "I understand why you want answers. I want a few myself, but I'll give you what I can. Though there are a few things I can't tell you...yet."

His response intrigued her, but she resisted pressing him for more information than he was willing to give— for the moment. As long as it didn't affect him working here, she didn't exactly *need* to know.

"I guess you could say that I see North Bank as a way to start fresh. I'm twenty-five and don't really know where my life is heading. To me, that seems like a waste." He grinned. "During a call with Adam, he talked a bunch about this place and...yeah, he happened to mention that you had a 'world class' bakery—as he put it—" Another grin. "—and he recommended me coming down here. I took him up on it."

Margot took in the young man's story with a nod.

"Thanks for being frank with me. Do you want to own your own bakery someday?" She saw the question took him by surprise.

"I do." He sounded wary, like she'd just read his mind.

"I talk to Adam too."

"That dog." He laughed, shaking his head. "Nah, it's good. I would have expected you to check me out beforehand and I'm glad that Adam vouched for me."

"This is all helpful for me to know." She nodded once, then surveyed the kitchen. "Okay. Back to work."

"Mrs. Durand?"

"Yes?"

"Thanks for taking a chance on me."

"Sure thing, Dex. And one more thing?"

"Anything," he said, his face registering honesty.

"Call me Margot."

They worked hard through the morning and she showed him more of how her business was run. By the early afternoon when Rosie came in, they were ahead of schedule and she started to see the potential for having an assistant. Not so much that she could take time off, but more so that she could do the things she'd been putting off. Planning out further than just the next few months. Have more interaction with her customers. It all gave her a rosy glow to the day, until she got the text from Tamera.

THERE'S BEEN ANOTHER MURDER.

CHAPTER 10

MARGOT WALKED the few blocks to Grant Park where the body had been found. Despite the fact that the scene was closed off, she risked coming to the front of the onlookers where the bright yellow tape stretched across the entrance.

"Stay back, please," an officer said. He was younger, newer to the area, but if she remembered correctly, his last name was Smith.

She'd just made it to the front when she spotted Adam. He saw her and shook his head, a slight smile on his lips.

"Smith," he said, coming forward. The young deputy looked up to him.

"Sir?"

"Let that one through," he said, pointing to Margot.

"Yes, sir. This way, ma'am," he said, helping her under the yellow tape.

A few reporters tossed out questions for Adam but he

ignored them, directing Margot to the shade of a large oak tree but not near where she assumed the body was.

"Why are you here, Margot? No, scratch that question. *How* did you find out about this?"

She grinned, knowing that he wasn't really angry at her for being there.

"Tamera was on a run this morning and saw the police cars. Heard from someone about what had happened. She messaged me. She wants to know if they are connected and, if so, if George will be released."

"And you just had to come by and see."

Margot shrugged, trying to look innocent. "I knew it couldn't hurt."

"Um huh." He shook his head, hands sliding to his hips as he looked back to where the body lay covered by a sheet. "I'm going to hazard a guess that this is not associated with the body found in Tamera's shop."

"What makes you say that?"

Adam roughed a hand over his jaw, the stubble there evidence that he had been called to the scene early that morning.

"The MO is way different and…" He trailed off and looked down at her. "I shouldn't be telling you any of this."

She offered him a shy smile. "If it's any consolation, I promise not to mention anything you've said—or will say—to anyone else."

He narrowed his eyes in thought for a moment, then nodded as if in agreement with her.

"This scene was…messy. This was no murder by

poisoning. And, while that's not conclusive evidence, it just *looks* different. In fact, it looks familiar."

"How so?"

"Remember how I told you I was working with my brother up in D.C. on a few cases?"

"Yes, I remember you had mentioned that at the beginning of summer."

"We actually worked a few that involved Victor Carow."

"Wait, the man who Mark Jennings was going to testify against?"

"You mean the *drug lord?* And yes, the very same man. Well, I should say his group. They have a certain way of… disposing of someone who has crossed them. It's part of the reason why I don't think Mark was killed by Carow's associates, but that remains to be seen."

"What do you mean?"

"This murder—it's got Carow's name all over it. Whoever he gets to do his bidding has a certain style. I won't say more, but the timing is odd. First Jennings is killed here and now this man? I don't like how all of this is coming together. We're in North Bank, for goodness sake. It's supposed to be Small Town America here."

Margot shivered despite the warmth of the sun and wrapped her arms around herself. "What do you think is really going on here?"

"I don't know," Adam said, his frown deepening. "But I've got to get back to the scene. Remember. Not a word."

She nodded in agreement and he saw her back under the yellow tape. As Margot walked away from the scene of the crime, she couldn't help but wonder what was going on in North Bank just like Adam had pointed out. This wasn't some hot bed of crime. It was a retirement community with a large senior population. Sure, they were close to the city, but why here?

The questions only managed to mount up in her mind, growing larger and larger until she couldn't think straight. The one thing she *did* know was that her friend needed her and she was going to be there for her.

~

AFTER MAKING a drive by of Tamera's house, Margot circled the large residential block and came back around to park far down the street. As she did, she noticed a dark-colored SUV she'd briefly seen on her first drive by. The outline of the driver was evident even from a distance. He looked to be a large man but she couldn't see more than that because of the tint of the windows.

The thing that was odd to her was that he had the windows rolled up and, in the ten minutes it had taken her to circle the block—due to a red light and a few pedestrian crossings—the person was still there.

At any other time, she may not have noticed the vehicle or the man in it, but her senses were on high alert. Not to mention the fact that the SUV looked like it could have been the one that ran them off the road the night before.

Her mouth instantly went dry at the memory of the headlights glaring and the speed at which they'd been driving over the massively high bridge only feet from flying over the side. If she could get close enough, would she see paint on the man's bumper?

Margot slid her hand into her purse and pulled out the mini-Taser she now carried almost everywhere with her. With her Krav Maga skills and this handy contraption, she felt secure. Armed with it in one hand and her phone in the other, she decided to approach the SUV. Chances were it was someone waiting to pick someone up and her fear was for nothing. She'd rather make a fool of herself. All she had to do was get close enough to get a good look at the license plate and maybe the face of the person in the vehicle.

She slipped down the tree-lined street, hiding behind bushes as they were available. Since she'd parked so far away, she had considerable ground to make up. But soon Tamera's house came into view as did the SUV parked only a few cars from Tamera's front door. Unfortunately, the person in the SUV had all but backed up into the car behind them, which made it impossible for Margot to see the back license plate.

She paused, covered by a large hydrangea bush, and peered through the leaves. She saw movement in the car and what looked like a flash of glass. Binoculars? Was he spying on Tamera? The feeling of foreboding increased. From the SUV's vantage point, they would be able to see all of the front windows of Tamera's house.

Making up her mind, Margot slipped from behind the tree and tried to duck-walk toward the car. She was almost to the car parked right behind when the sound of barking shattered the stillness of the neighborhood.

A light tan blur launched itself at Margot who, in her surprise, let out a cry as Mr. Puggles attacked her face with licks.

Lights blinked on at the same time the engine of the SUV roared to life. The next second, the sound of crunching plastic and metal accompanied the SUV's hasty exit from the tight parking spot. The driver had backed into the car and then rammed the bumper of the car in front of him in his hurry to escape.

The sound of screeching tires was the last thing Margot saw. She ground her teeth, angry at herself for not getting his license plate number, but she'd been so shocked at his hasty retreat from the parking space and the shock of having a dog in her arms that she hadn't been able to memorize it or even capture a picture of the plate. Some detective she was turning out to be.

"Margot, what is going on?" Tamera was running from the house to her, eyes wide in surprise.

Margot pulled herself off the ground and brushed off stray bits of grass. "What's going on is I think I just saw the person who tried to run us off the road yesterday. And I let him get away."

"What?"

Margot explained how she'd seen the man and how she assumed he had been spying on Tamera, to which her friend shivered and looked over her shoulder as if he could be right behind her.

"I don't like this one bit. Another murder and now this? Who is that man?"

"Did you see him?"

"Not really. He was wearing dark sunglasses and had dark hair—I think. He drove off so fast and there was a glare in the window."

Margot stared in the direction he'd driven in. "Well, at least we can give a statement about the car. Want to go down to the police station with me?"

"Why don't you call Adam?" Tamera stopped and picked up Mr. Puggles, who squirmed to be let free again.

"I have a feeling he'll be busy at the crime scene for a while. Then you can stop by to see George. He's still not released?"

Margot saw the stormy look gather in Tamer's eyes. "No. And I've just about had it."

"Come on. Let's put Mr. Puggles back inside and head to the station." She surveyed the street one more time then said, more to herself than her friend who was already nearing her home, "I have a feeling there are more than a few puzzles going on here."

CHAPTER 11

AFTER MARGOT and Tamera gave a revised statement about the vehicle from the previous night to a deputy on duty, they walked across the street to the jail where George was being held. It was adjacent to the courthouse and, while not high security, still had a sterile, cold feel about it. They were shown into a room with a metal table and three chairs, only a small window high on the wall and encased in bars and shatterproof glass giving off dim light.

As they sat, Margot turned to her friend. "Are you sure you want me in here? I can give you guys some time to talk."

"No." Tamera clasped Margot's hand. "I want you here. Besides, I think it's time I asked George why he came back early and I want you here with me."

When George was shown in, he sat down in the chair facing the two women and reached across the table for Tamera's hands. "Tam," he said, his voice scratchy.

Margot saw tears enter her friend's eyes and she again realized how difficult this had to be for her. Not only was her husband *still* in jail, she had reason to believe he had lied to her.

"How are you, sweetie?"

Tamera sniffed. "Not good, George. I want this all to be over."

"I know, honey, me too. Me too." He patted her hand gently and Margot felt a wave of longing wash through her. She and Julian had had this kind of love. And though he'd been gone almost five years now, she could still almost feel his touch in rare moments of quiet when she closed her eyes.

But that was in the past and she needed to focus on the present. And if she was going to save her friend some of the heartache she was facing, Margot had to begin the difficult conversation.

"George," she said, hating to interrupt their moment but knowing it was necessary, "I've got some difficult questions to ask you."

He turned to her, surprise on his sharp features. "What do you mean, Margot?"

Margot glanced toward Tamera and then back at her husband. "We know that you didn't come back for a work meeting."

The color drained from George's already pale features. "W-what do you mean?"

"I called your boss, George. When I mentioned the meeting, he didn't know what I was talking about."

The silence dropped heavily between them as George's

gaze drilled into the metal tabletop. Finally, after a few moments, he took in a deep breath and looked up.

"I suppose I should have come out with all of this long before now, but I was...I don't know. I suppose I was hoping it wouldn't have to come up."

"What do you mean?"

His brow furrowed more deeply and he turned his gaze to Tamera. "I should have told you before we got married. I was going to...but then I thought it was behind me and it wouldn't affect our lives. But then...then it did and it was too late and..."

"George," Margot pushed into the one-sided conversation. "Start from the beginning. Let us know so we can help you."

He looked at Margot for a long time then nodded, turning his focus back to his wife.

"You knew that I was married before, but what I didn't tell you was that I had a daughter during that time." Tamera merely nodded, not wanting to interrupt the flow of her husband's confession. "She's a sweet girl. Her name is Sarah, and I would do anything to protect her."

Margot felt her stomach twist into knots. *Anything?*

"But by the time she graduated high school, I had been out of her life for a few years, estranged from her mother, and I'd barely seen her. I did hear stories of how she wasn't doing well, but I didn't even know how to find her." He let out a heavy sigh. "Finally, when my private practice was established, that was before I moved to Washington, D.C., I got an email from her. She was in some deep trouble and needed money. We met and, as I talked with her, I could see she wanted out. She'd been involved in all sorts of terrible things and just needed a new start. So, I helped. I got her out of the situation, moved her across the country to Virginia, and she started over."

"Wait," Tamera interrupted. "Sarah. As in…Sarah Newman?"

"You know her?" Margot wasn't following.

"That's where things get complicated." George seemed to deflate before Margot's eyes. "We hadn't been close and just because I helped her, didn't mean our relationship was healed. I was satisfied to know she was safe. But… then I was offered a job at my current company, a big step up for me, and came to find out that it was due to my daughter, who had married the head partner's son."

The pieces began to click. This was why Tamera had known his daughter's name. Was it possible she had even met his daughter at an event? Margot looked to her friend and saw an expression of pain and confusion on her delicate features.

"When I came east, we met and decided it was best for us not to mention our familial ties. She had reinvented herself and taken another name before marrying Trevor—my boss's son—and she said that Trevor knew nothing of her past. I wasn't about to ruin what little relationship we did have, and besides, I wanted my daughter to succeed so I kept my mouth shut."

"But someone found out," Margot said, almost to herself.

George's eyes snapped to hers. "Yes. How did you know?"

"Because I'm beginning to see that there are several things going on here, and this is only part of it. You were —or are—being blackmailed, aren't you?"

"I am." George looked shocked that she knew.

Margot thought of the regular payments George had taken out of his account. "What happened when you came back early from the honeymoon trip?"

He sighed heavily. "Years ago, I had been contacted by a Harry Beakman."

Margot's mind flicked back to the email address she'd seen. *Beaky123*.

"He had gone to high school with Sarah and apparently fallen in love with her, but she'd never returned the feelings. When he came on hard times years out of high school, he looked her up. Somehow he found who she used to associate with and followed her trail to Virginia. That's when he came to me saying he'd ruin Sarah's new life unless I gave him a little something to tide him over."

George ran a hand over his face, the weariness of all that had happened taking its toll on him.

"At the time, I wasn't really sure what to do. I wanted my little girl to succeed and I was afraid that Harry showing up on her doorstep and telling her new husband what she'd been involved in in the past would ruin everything. So I paid him. He went away and I thought I'd seen the last of him, but that was too good to be true. He started to show up every few months like clockwork. He never demanded so much that I couldn't pay him, but I knew he'd be coming back."

"Oh, George," Tamera said, grasping his hand. "Why didn't you tell me?"

"That's just it." He locked gazes with her. "When I met you, my life changed. Everything changed. I not only fell in love with you but I wanted you to meet Sarah and *know* she was my daughter. I wanted to tell you everything. I was going to—on our honeymoon in Hawaii—but then I got an email from Harry. I knew if I was going to tell you, I wanted to be able to say that it would never be a problem again. So I took more money than he'd asked for and went to meet him."

Margot thought of what Adam had told her about the larger withdrawal he'd made. The facts were lining up.

"I met with him and told him this would be the last of it. I was going to give him the money and then I wasn't going to give him any more. He threatened me, told me he'd go public with everything, but I'd already fessed up to Sarah and she'd agreed it was time. She was going to tell Trevor soon too. There really wasn't anything left for Harry to hold over me."

"What did he say?" Margot prompted.

"He got mad. We'd met at the park down the street from the shop, and he started throwing his hands up and arguing with me. Something snapped in me. I saw how foolish this all had been. I know that Trevor loves my little girl and I know that Tam loves me. There was no reason to keep secrets. So instead, I said forget it, pocketed the money, and walked off. That's when I stopped by the shop to get the glue stick since I was already in town. I went by the bank on my way back and deposited the money, then went home."

Margot leaned back. It fit. All of it. She needed to tell Adam that they were holding the wrong man.

～

STRONG HANDS CAUGHT her as she rushed from the room and straight into Adam's firm chest.

"Wha— Adam!"

He looked down at her, his gaze narrowing. "How did you know?"

She blinked. "Know? Know what?"

"About all of that?"

"Oh." She looked through the viewing window.

"I got your text," he said by way of explaining.

"I *didn't* know." She bit her lip, wondering what Tamera would think of her sending a text to Adam about meeting with George. "I just thought...well, I knew he hadn't told the truth about coming back to meet with his boss and—"

"Stop right there. Why didn't you tell me you were coming to talk with George?"

"I sent you a text." Margot bit her lip. She knew she'd messed up. She hadn't waited for him.

Adam shook his head. "If we're doing this—" He gestured between the two of them. She wanted to ask him to clarify exactly what *this* was, but he kept going. "—then we need to tell each other everything. Especially about important conversations like this." He pointed into the room.

"I didn't want to betray George's trust."

"I get it." He let out a sigh. "It's inadmissible but it's information I need so I can hone in on the *right* person."

"I know. And we'll persuade him to talk with you."

He stared off into space for a moment before he looked back down at her. "I put out an announcement to all of the patrol units in town and got a call from someone on the west side of town. Someone saw the SUV, right down to the paint on the front and back bumpers. Got a license plate number on it too. Seems like this Harry guy is the one who's been following you and Tamera."

"What?" Margot tried to reason through all of this and Adam's change of subject. So Harry hadn't gotten his money and now he was terrorizing Tamera? Was he doing it to send George a message? Seemed risky, but someone in need of money could stoop to something foolish like this.

"After this—" Adam motioned toward the two-way mirror into the room she'd just come from. "And your run-in with him, I think we have enough to bring Mr. Beakman in for questioning."

"I'm sorry, Adam," she said, resting her hand on his arm. "I really wasn't trying to keep anything from you."

"I know." He roughed his hand over his jaw again. "I'm just overly tired. This case—or cases, as it's turning out to be—are doing a number on our small staff."

Margot felt so sorry for her friend and the weight of

responsibility that rested on his shoulders. They had to solve these cases—and quickly.

"We know George didn't kill Mark—"

"Or we're reasonably certain," Adam cut in.

"Right, so where does that leave us."

Adam huffed out a sigh. "I think it puts us back to a Carow sympathizer. Maybe a paid hit?"

"But it's clear the murderer wanted us to think it was George."

"Explain."

"Aside from the obvious—the body being found in the shop—I think Mrs. Henderson saw Mark go into the shop. Remember how Rachel said she loaned Mark her fedora? George almost always wears one, so it was as if Mark was being set up to look like George. Meanwhile, the killer waits for him in a darkened shop and attacks him."

"Making all leads point to George."

"Yes."

"So that leaves us with someone who knows George, knows he wears fedoras, and has access to the shop."

"That could be any number of people. Well, minus the access to the shop. That wouldn't be easy."

Adam nodded just as footsteps came down the hall toward them.

"Chief," he said, his voice sounding strained.

"Eastwood," the police chief said. He was a tall man in his mid-fifties with graying hair and piercing blue eyes that seemed to look through a person. He was rail thin and stood with his hands on his hips as he first looked at the two-way mirror and then at Margot before resting his gaze back on Adam. "Want to tell me what's going on here?"

Adam filled the man in with a concise wrap-up of what they'd just discovered. He finished by saying, "So we need to figure out what the link is between North Bank and Mark Jennings. Among other things," Adam trailed off, grimacing. Margot assumed he hated how vague it all sounded.

"And you, Mrs. Durand?" the chief said. He had only just transferred to North Bank around the time that Julian had been killed so her interaction with the hardened man had been limited.

"I was, um…" she fumbled for words.

"She was helping me." Adam stood a little straighter as if expecting lash back from this.

"In what capacity?" the man barked.

"She knows Tamera and George and was able to uncover the blackmail going on."

The chief's eyes narrowed again as he turned to look at her. "I won't underestimate the observations of an outsider. God knows our small staff could use a consultant or two. You run everything through Adam, you hear?"

"Y-Yes, sir," she responded. Had he really used the word consultant? Then again, he hadn't called *her* one…yet.

"Keep up the good work," the man growled over his shoulder as he turned back down the hallway.

"What…"

When Margot looked up at Adam, he had a strange expression on his face but it slipped away as soon as she rested her hand on his arm again.

"Does this mean you can take me back to the crime scene?"

He blinked. "What?"

"I need to see the inside of the shop again. I think we've missed something."

Adam let out a long breath. "Sure. But I'm making an executive order that we stop by The Coffee Kraft first or else I'm not going to make it."

CHAPTER 12

AFTER TELLING Tamera that they were going back to her shop, she handed over her keys and said she would wait there for George to be released. Margot tried to warn her that she could be waiting a long time, but her friend said she didn't mind. She told her that if they needed to get home, they could call a cab or another friend but that she knew Margot would need to check on her shop as well.

Reluctant but knowing her friend needed to stay, she took Tamera's keys and met Adam in the hall. He said he'd swing by The Coffee Kraft and get them both coffee and that they could meet up outside of the Craft Boutique in ten minutes.

The trip downtown took seven minutes, giving Margot just enough time to park near her shop and walk up the street to meet Adam in front of the boutique, the yellow tape still sealing it off from public entrance.

The scene had already been picked apart and documented, the tape only a precaution in case they needed to gain access again. Adam opened the door with his key and they stepped inside.

Everything felt—and looked—the same as it had when Margot had come in that night with Tamera. Everything except for the body, of course. Something she was grateful not to see again. A shiver at the mere thought made her wrap her arms around herself.

"You okay?" Adam asked. His penetrating gaze didn't miss anything.

"Just remembering the other night."

"I'm so sorry you had to go through that."

She gave him a halfhearted smile. "I would have preferred not to walk in on a body lying on the floor of my best friend's shop too," she quipped. "But thanks."

"So," he said, holding his hands behind his back and looking around. "What is it that the great Margot Durand saw that she can't put her finger on?"

His light tone made all of this feel more normal than it should have, but she ignored the second shudder that threatened to course through her.

"I'm not sure." She was still shocked that Chief Heartland hadn't dressed her down for poking her nose into Adam's case. Was it the fact that she had helped with the previous case at the beginning of the summer? Or was he so desperate to wrap this up that he welcomed her help? The moment she gave space to that thought, she dismissed it. John Heartland was anything but desperate. No, there was something else that she couldn't put her finger on but she wasn't going to spend time thinking about it. Not now when they were in the midst of an investigation.

She circled the area where Mark Jennings had been found. Nothing around him was disturbed. He had either fallen, or been placed, in one of the only areas where his large frame wouldn't hinder the already cramped aisles of the boutique. Coincidence? Or careful planning? But why was it so important that nothing be disturbed? If you had murdered someone, organization seemed to be the last thing you would worry about.

Margo closed her eyes and tried again to remember what had felt off about the space to her. She was certain it was a subconscious feeling that had seeped in to her conscious thought. Those annoying types of feelings that you *knew* existed but disappeared when you tried to put your finger on them.

She sidestepped and then stopped, standing up straight. "That's why," she uttered to herself.

"What? What's why?"

"I wondered why he had been placed here, but I think I know why."

"Care to enlighten this extremely tired detective?"

She looked up at Adam and noticed the deep bags under his eyes and the way his hair was ruffled on the side, probably from when he'd been dragged from sleep to come down to the park. He was guzzling coffee now, but she knew only true rest would make him feel better.

"Nothing is disturbed, and I thought that was on purpose—it may very well be—but look at the sight line."

He joined her, looking where she indicated with her arm. "This aisle goes straight to the back door. Just that one rolling cart that Tam uses for go-backs is in the way. Move it, and you've got a direct path from the back door to here."

Adam nodded. "I can see that."

Margot stepped forward and knelt by the wheeled cart. "I'm not an expert, but it looks like the indentations are slightly off. Granted, it's a wheeled cart so we don't know if it's been moved recently or not. It's just at theory."

"So where does this theory get you?"

"To the back door." She stepped around the cart. "It wasn't forced, was it?"

"No."

"Then…" Her thoughts trailed off and she pulled out her phone.

"Who are you calling?"

"Tam. Hold on." She put the call through but her friend didn't pick up. "Of course. She's probably got her phone on silent." Instead, she tapped in a quick text.

"What are you asking her?"

"I'm asking her who has keys."

"It's in the report," he said, scrunching up his nose in thought. "I believe she said herself, George, you, and her lawyer in case of emergencies."

"Well, I want to double-check. It's possible someone had a key made—somehow. Or they are really good at picking a lock, but I just don't think they would have had time."

"You think they got in with a key."

"I do."

Adam shrugged. "Beats me how."

She nodded and did one more once-over of the room. It was still there. The feeling that something was out of place or missing persisted but without being able to put her finger on it, it was pointless to stand around waiting.

Adam's phone shattered the silence. He sent her an apologetic look as he slid his finger across the screen. "Eastwood."

BACK AT THE BAKERY, Margot slumped into her desk chair. It had been an incredibly long, confusing, and emotional day. Thankfully, when she stepped into the shop, the smells of sweets and the cooling air of the fans worked to calm her frayed nerves.

"Mrs. Durand?" a voice said from her door.

She looked up at her new assistant, a bit of flour covering his white apron but looking no worse for wear.

"Hey, Dexter. I'm so sorry for leaving so abruptly today."

He grinned, holding up his hands. "Not at all what I was going to say. I actually was going to ask if you wanted me to take care of tomorrow's baking on my own?"

His offer took her by surprise. He was a good baker, she'd seen enough in the last few days to know that she trusted his expertise, but she wasn't ready to let him take over completely. And certainly not as a temporary helper.

"Thanks for the offer. I really appreciate it—"

"But no thanks?" he said with a smile.

She reciprocated with a smile of her own. "It has nothing to do with your talent, just so we're clear. But I'll be in in the morning."

"Sure, just wanted to offer."

"Maybe I'll take you up on that someday."

He grinned and nodded. "I hope that you do."

"Feel free to head out. I'll close up."

He nodded and started to untie his apron as he left her office doorway. She checked her email quickly, replying to a few actionable notes, and then closed down her computer. She'd do a double-check of her inventory and then close up.

The silence of the bakery sobered her thoughts. She missed her days here. She hadn't seen Bentley nearly all week and, after getting used to seeing him almost every day, that was a big change in her schedule. She missed it. Missed the baking.

Right then she knew she couldn't go home yet. She would make something—anything—to give her hands something to do. She had a feeling it would help to calm her nerves and focus her thoughts.

Pulling out the ingredients she'd need, she set to work making her famous *religieuse,* which was two layers of choux pastry filled with white cream and topped with a dark chocolate icing and piped vanilla cream, emphasizing the look of the nun's habit for which the pastry was named. They were her favorite things to make and she tended to only make them weekly due to her detail-oriented focus and their time-consuming nature, but tonight seemed as good as any to splurge. She would freeze them and sell them at a discount the next day, but it would be worth it.

As she worked, her thoughts wandered back to Tamera's shop. What was out of place? It was driving her mad.

Her phone rang just as she was filling the pastry with cream. Pushing her hair back with the back of her hand, she rushed to where her phone was plugged into the outlet and used a knuckle to tap the answer and then speaker buttons.

"Margie?"

"Hey, Adam," she said, brushing the same unruly hair back again.

"You didn't go home yet, did you?"

When they had parted ways from the boutique, Adam had been heading to meet up with the M.E. about the body found in the park and she'd come to the shop.

"No, not yet. I'm here at the shop."

"Good. Wait for me to come get you."

She frowned. "Why? I've got Tamera's car."

"I'll escort you home. I'm sure you want to know what I found out at the M.E.'s office."

"You sure know how to entice a girl."

His full-bodied laugh sent a smile across her lips. "You know it. Be there in fifteen minutes?"

She looked over at the counter and grimaced. "Make it twenty and you have a deal."

"Got it." He hung up without preamble, but she was used to that. Julian had done the same thing.

Part of her felt bad for the feelings that were ever so

slowly beginning to emerge toward Adam. It had been years since her husband had passed away, but that didn't mean that she could just pick up and move on. And what would Julian think of her and Adam? They weren't anything more than friends now...but was there something else there? Could there be? She was fairly certain Adam wanted there to be.

Sighing, she went back to working on her pastries and was soon drawn back to the boutique. As she switched out her pastry bag for the light purple icing she would use to add a small bouquet of flowers to the front of the nun-like pastry, she stopped, hand in midair.

Flowers. Purple flowers. That was it!

Piping on the rest of the flowers at lightning speed, she left one *religieuse* on the counter for Adam and put the rest in the industrial-sized freezer. Then she rushed to her phone and fired off a text to Tamera.

Waiting impatiently for the reply, she went about cleaning up the kitchen and getting everything ready for the next morning. She was just finishing up when she heard the ding of her phone.

Tamera's text confirmed what she'd remembered.

"OH, I was hoping you'd been baking," Adam said as he stepped through the back door into the kitchen and made a beeline to the *religieuse*. "These are my favorite!"

"You say that about every one of my pastries."

He gave her an impish grin. "Can't I like more than one?"

She laughed but grew serious. "Adam, I finally realized what was off in the boutique."

He paused mid-bite, his eyes growing wide. "Waa?" he mumbled around the pastry.

"I almost didn't see it because it had been changed, but then it was all so clear when I was piping on the frosting and—"

"Hold up," Adam said, licking that very same frosting from his lips. "What in the world are you talking about, Margot?"

Blushing, she realized she hadn't explained herself well at all. "Sorry. So, I remembered there used to be a painting of a foxglove field hanging on the wall right next to where the body lay. It didn't stand out to me—or Tamera—because that exhibit isn't curated by Tam, she lets the artist do it. But I *know* the foxglove painting was there when I checked on the shop a few days before Tam came back because I remember thinking I might purchase it for the shop."

"It's not there now."

"No." Margot thought back to their trip to the store that day. "It was replaced by a sunset picture of the Potomac. It's lovely, but *not* the picture that was there before."

"So the killer took the painting?"

Margot hesitated. This was where she stepped into speculation rather than fact. "I'm not sure, but the painting was of foxglove—"

"The poison that killed Mark Jennings."

"Yes."

"And the killer didn't want to tip us off?" Adam said, though she knew he wasn't serious.

"What if the killer *was* the artist?"

"What would make you say that?"

"I don't know him well, but I did meet the artist, Mr. Jerold Bascom, at his opening. Everyone along Main Street came by to support him. He told a few stories about his works and I remember one of them being the large foxglove field behind his home."

"So this man has access to foxglove."

"Yes, but at the same time, why risk removing the painting? Unless you had one to replace it with and a valid reason to replace it? Jerold could have used the poison, seen the painting, and replaced it just in case it tipped anyone off to him. Since Tam doesn't keep tabs on what he has in the shop, no one would really notice it had been changed."

"It seems too circumstantial for my liking."

"Right," Margot said, walking toward her phone, "but I've got an idea."

"Uh-oh," Adam said, humor lacing his voice.

"See?" she said, holding out her phone for him to see. "That's him there. And, if I can take this to Barbara at the Library, she can confirm that it was *him* who was looking into the whole Victor Carow thing."

"That still is a long way from proving anything."

"I know," Margot said, feeling her shoulders drop. "But it's the only lead we have."

Adam nodded. "All right. Let's go talk to Barbara and see what she says. Then maybe we can do some research of our own."

Feeling bolstered by Adam's encouragement, she nodded and reached for her purse. "All right, Watson. Let's go."

"Nope," he said, narrowing his gaze at her.

"What?" she said.

"We both know that I'm Sherlock in this duo."

CHAPTER 13

WHEN THEY REACHED THE LIBRARY, Barbara had already gone home but Adam was able to flash his badge and convince Wilhelmina to give them her address. She opened the door, leaning heavily on her crutches, and looked surprised.

"What are you doing here, Margot?"

"Ma'am," Adam said, pulling out his credentials again. "I'm Detective Adam Eastwood with the police department. I'd like to ask you a few questions."

Barbara's eyebrows rose and she glanced at Margot again. "And she's here…."

"Because she's helping me with the investigation."

Margot pressed her lips together, trying hard not to smile knowing that admission had to cost him.

"Oh, I see." Her expression brightened immediately. "That's lovely for you, Margot! Come on in."

Barbara directed them to a small sitting area and

landed with a grunt in an old recliner. Then she said, "How can I help you?"

Margot noticed, again with a barely concealed smile, that Barbara directed her attention fully toward her. "Um, well, remember when I came by the other day and asked about the man who you'd helped research Victor Carow?"

"Oh yes, I remember." Barbara's smile widened.

"I was wondering if you recognized the man you saw in this photo." Without indicating anyone specifically to Barbara, she handed over her phone.

The woman used her fingers to zoom in on the screen and peered very closely through everyone's photo. "Oh, you look lovely here. Turquoise really is your color, Margot."

Adam shot her a look that clearly said, *Can we speed this up?* But Margot merely smiled.

"Why thank you, Barbara." She was enjoying this too much.

"Well, I looked through the whole photo to be sure, but that's him."

Margot's heart beat more rapidly. "Which one?"

"The tall guy standing on the end there. He was the one who came in and who I helped. Nice man, but quiet."

"You're sure?" Margot silently berated herself for not having asked about the man's age. The major difference between Jerold and George was their major age difference, but Barbara wouldn't have known to clarify.

"Positive."

Margot met Adam's gaze and he nodded once, letting her know that he realized what this meant. After he took the lead, asking Barbara a few more questions, they excused themselves and headed back to Adam's car.

"She pointed him out. It's him—Jerold Bascom."

Adam nodded. "While she was looking, I shot off a text to a friend in D.C. He's doing some research on Mr. Bascom and should get back to me any minute now."

"I just can't believe Mr. Bascom would do something like this." Margot clicked her seatbelt and Adam pulled into traffic. "Where are we going?"

"My place," Adam said, his eyes on the road. It was nearing five o'clock and traffic was picking up. Though 'traffic' in North Bank hardly constituted that much worry. Still, the streets would clog soon and she was sure that, rather than going back across town to the police station, Adam's house would make a good staging ground for whatever they planned next.

Pulling into his garage, they entered through the doorway that led into the laundry room and then the kitchen. A loud bark preceded scratching claws and then the impossibly large body of Adam's Great Dane, Clint.

"Hey, Clinty boy," Margot said, bending down. With one solid lick to the cheek, she jerked back with a laugh. "Well, that's a hello."

"He's got good taste in women," Adam said, wagging his eyebrows at her.

She laughed again and shook her head. "Well, if he was the *real* Clint Eastwood…"

"I know, I know," Adam said, holding up his hands. "He just happens to have two too many feet, eh? Hold on, let me take him out back."

The duo disappeared out the back sliding door and Margot made herself at home on Adam's large couch. She'd been in his home a few times, mostly for large BBQs he hosted due to the size of his back yard, but now she looked at it through a different lens. Through Adam her friend—maybe more than friend—lens.

He had several pictures of himself with his brother and parents on the mantle over an oft-used fireplace. Across from her, tall bookshelves were lined with everything from cheap paperbacks to large law tomes. If she remembered correctly, he had started off as a law student before changing focus. Now she wanted to hear more about that story and more from his past.

But her mind jerked back to the present when Adam's phone, abandoned on the kitchen counter when he went to take Clint out, started ringing. She bolted up from the couch and grabbed it just as Adam came in the door. The two nearly collided but he managed to catch her before she ran headlong into him while simultaneously answering the phone as if nothing had happened. He was smooth, she'd admit that.

Clint bounded up to her, looking to give another slobbery kiss, but he settled on a good, behind-the-ears scratching instead. She tried her best not to listen in on Adam's conversation, but it was nearly impossible since he was standing right next to her. As if sensing her dilemma, he beckoned her over to a barstool at the counter and pulled the phone away from his ear, tapping the speaker button.

"Can you say that again, Gary?"

"You got it, man," a man said, his accent immediately placing him from Maryland. "I ran the details on the name you sent me. Seems your guy has some very interesting ties to Victor Carow."

Margot almost gasped out loud but managed to cover her shock with a hand over her mouth. Her eyes met Adam's, but he looked back down at the phone as if to help himself focus.

"Go on," he said.

"I contacted a friend over at the DEA—"

Margot mentally filled in the initials: Drug Enforcement Administration.

"And he says that this Jerold guy is on a watch list or two."

"Why is that?" Adam's forehead showed his intense concentration. Margot wondered if he was kicking himself for not knowing that a man on some DEA watch list was living in his jurisdiction.

"Jerold Bascom is the grandfather of Thomas Bascom."

"Thomas," Adam said, "I recognize that name."

"I thought you might from your time up here. He's a low level player in the Victor Carow operation. No one that would especially draw your attention, but that's not surprising."

"Why is that?" Adam took the words right out of Margot's thoughts.

"Because he's not the important guy. Honestly, he's nothing. A dealer, but he's got no inside information. Nothing that would make you take notice—except for his family tie to Jerold Bascom."

Now Margot was confused. How would a simple drug dealer—though she feared that *no* drug dealer was truly simple—get wrapped up in a murder of this magnitude? Had he needed to prove something to his boss? Or had he been a fall guy? Or had he even been involved?

"The real interesting part becomes clear when you do a little family history." Gary chuckled. "I feel like a regular historian."

"Must be nice," Adam said, "but get to the point."

"Okay, okay, hold your horses."

Margot glanced at Adam. She knew he wasn't an impatient man, but he was a man on a mission. He had a murder to solve and she could see that the stress, and lack of sleep, were taking their toll.

"Jerold Bascom, though not related in any way to Carow's drug ring as far as we can tell, *did* go to high school with none other than Archie Shaw."

Margot had no idea what significance that held, but Adam stood up from where he'd been bent over the phone and ran a hand through his hair. And, likely for her benefit, he said, "Victor Carow's grandfather."

"Ding-ding-ding, you've got it."

"So, what…" Adam started pacing now. "Jerold took the hit on Mark Jennings so that he could help his grandson? Bring him up in the ranks? What's DEA saying?"

"They've got a guy on the inside of Carow's ring and he says that a deal was made. Jennings for Thomas."

Margot stumbled back a step, hardly believing what she heard. Jerold Bascom had agreed to *murder* a man who had turned witness so that he could save his grandson. It was almost impossible to believe. Then again, she barely knew Jerold. The little conversation they'd held had centered around his artwork and that was it. He wasn't like the other retirees or those at the senior center who made a point to stop by the bakery and get to know her. He didn't go to any of the town's gatherings, as far as she had seen, and he wasn't active outside of putting his paintings up in Tamera's shop.

"And the recent victim?"

Gary sighed. "My guy thinks it was a warning, but unrelated."

The two men kept talking, but Margot lost track of the conversation.

What would Tamera say to all of this? And George? His involvement had to be accidental, didn't it? Or was he merely a scapegoat?

But the fact remained. Jerold had ties to Victor Carow and he had keys to the shop. Distantly, Margot knew that Adam had hung up with Gary and was now on the phone to the chief. He was relaying all of the information and getting men on tracking Jerold down, but all she could think about was how convoluted it all was. If what Gary said was true, he'd done it to save his grandson, but that didn't excuse his actions. He'd still murdered a good man, a man who could have sealed the fate of Victor Carow.

She slumped back onto the barstool and dropped her head into her hands. How could this possibly end well?

CHAPTER 14

"I NEED TO GO."

Margot looked up, her eyes locking with Adam's. "Aren't you going to wait for backup?"

His lips pressed into a thin line and he glanced to the side before answering. "I should have seen this connection earlier."

"How?" Margot placed her hand on Adam's forearm, hoping he would listen to reason. "You couldn't have known. You're not a mind reader."

"Either way, I still need to go. I need to make sure that Jerold isn't skipping town as we speak. Then again, he's had ample time. I doubt he's still even here."

Margot ran through the facts. If Jerold were certain that no one could tie him back to the murder, would he have left? Up until this point, the media had latched on to the idea that one of Victor Carow's men had murdered Mark Jennings. It made sense, knowing the importance of the trial and the violence Carow was known for—though not convicted of.

"He could still be here."

Adam paused at the sink where he was filling up a glass with water. "What makes you say that?"

"Look at it this way. Jerold isn't a spring chicken. He's lived in this community for many years and, while I don't know him well, I would assume he planned on living his days out here."

"He wouldn't wait around for us to find him, Margie."

"No, probably not, but he probably doesn't think he's even in the running as a suspect—and, up until a few hours ago, he would be right. It's such a new development that he could still be here. Besides, didn't you tell me that you thought the murder in the park was a Carow gang murder?"

"It was. I spoke with the M.E. and he confirmed the gang's mark on the body."

"See? That just fuels the idea that it was gang-related."

"There are a lot of holes in that theory," Adam said, though not unsympathetically.

"I know it, but to a seventy-five-year-old grandfather —or however old he is—it could be enough."

The first light of hope entered Adam's eyes at this. "Then I *really* need to go."

"Take me with you."

"Absolutely not."

"Adam..." She stood up and faced him, hands on her hips. "Do we need to review the facts here? He's not going to come after us with a gun. His weapon of choice was poison. Isn't that what most *women* kill with."

Adam grimaced but didn't reply.

"Besides, what will I do here?"

"Kiss Clint Eastwood?"

Margot rolled her eyes but had a feeling that was his way of agreeing. She waited, holding her breath.

"Okay," he finally said. "But there are ground rules and I want you to hear that you are *only* coming with me to stay in the car and *only* because I really don't think this grandfatherly Jerold Bascom—though a murderer—is going to come after us. Probably."

She smirked in triumph and handed him his keys.

Gary had transmitted Jerold's last known address to Adam's phone and, after double-checking with someone at the records office at the station, they set off toward Jerold's house.

Margot felt her stomach twist in knots. She wasn't exactly sure why she'd decided to come, but she had a feeling it was something of the investigator in her. She needed to see this through. She needed to know that they had found the right man.

When they turned down the street where Jerold's house was located, she was glad to see that most of the neighbors didn't seem to be home yet. Less prying eyes were a good thing in this nosy town. Really, she was thinking of the neighbors' safety.

Adam parked down the street a bit then looked toward her. "Backup is on its way, though they are stuck in some sort of traffic accident. Of all the days," he said, rolling his eyes.

"You're not going in there alone," she said, incredulous.

"Like you said, you don't think he's dangerous."

"No, but still..." Then the front door to a house next to Bascom's opened and an elderly woman walked out, her tiny Pomeranian trotting beside her. She wore a pink tracksuit and looked to be around the age they assumed Bascom was.

"I've got an idea," Margot said and was out of the car before Adam could tell her not to leave.

"Excuse me," she said, walking up to the woman. Adam joined her, looking uncomfortable and scanning the area.

"Hello," the older woman said, her dog sniffing at Adam's feet, no doubt smelling Clint.

"I was wondering if you could help me. I'm looking for a Jerold Bascom?" Adam flinched when she said the name out loud but she persisted. "I wanted to buy a painting from him, but I haven't been able to get in touch recently. I thought he lived along this street and I wanted to stop by."

"Oh yes," the woman said, nodding rapidly. "Jerold is my neighbor. His paintings are very nice, aren't they? Say, you look familiar?" She leaned toward Margot with pinched eyes.

"I've just got one of those faces," Margot said, laughing uncomfortably. "Have you seen him recently?"

"Who?" the woman said.

"Mr. Bascom."

"Oh," the woman laughed and yanked her dog closer to her. "Haven't seen him out in a few days. It's not unusual, though. Some days, he'll be in there for almost a week straight without leaving. Just gets his mail now and then. I'm sure he could use the company, dear." She laughed again, the sound raspy.

"So, you think he's home?"

"I'm sure of it. Saw him get the mail this morning. Hasn't been out since, though. His car's still there. Besides, I'd know if he left."

"Why is that?" *Besides the fact that you're nosy,* Margot thought with good humor.

"Because his car is in desperate need of a new muffler." She winked and then tugged at the small dog again. "We'd better be off. Good luck with your painting."

Margot forced a smile then looked at Adam, wondering what he thought of her investigative techniques. His look was hard to read but he nodded. "Smoothly done, Watson."

"Let's go," she said.

"Ah, nope. Nice try, but—"

"Come on, Adam. You heard what she said. He's practically a hermit. He's not going to come at us with guns blazing or—"

The distant sound of sirens caught their attention.

"I told them no sirens." Adam ground his teeth. "Come on."

Now Margot wanted to know what made him change his mind. She risked asking, "Really?"

"Yeah, don't want him escaping out the back."

Margot almost rolled her eyes, but she was getting what she wanted and wasn't about to risk that.

"But stay behind me. Got it?"

She nodded and they approached the house.

CHAPTER 15

THEY BYPASSED the front door and walked down the driveway, ducking under the large bay window, even though the curtains were drawn, and coming to a stop at the corner of the house that led to where Margot assumed the back door was.

Adam turned back to her. "I'm going to go around first; you follow but stay directly behind me. Okay?"

Margot nodded.

"Okay?" he repeated.

"Okay," Margot said, realizing he needed to hear her agree with him.

Then he slipped around the corner, gun drawn. She still wasn't sure if this situation warranted as much fear as she was giving it, but then again, Jerold *had* killed someone. It was just difficult for her to wrap her mind around the reality that he was a cold-blooded killer. The nice man who painted such serene landscapes.

She almost walked into Adam when he stopped at the

short row of three steps that led up to the back door. Only then did she notice that the door was open a few inches. Had Jerold escaped on foot? It seemed hardly likely knowing his age, but she supposed it *could* be possible.

Adam reached out at the same moment someone came rocketing out the back door. Margot shrieked, unable to help herself, and Adam went down. The man who had tackled him was unfamiliar to Margot. He looked like he was in his late thirties or early forties, though she only saw the side of his face.

Before she could do anything to help Adam, the man shoved up and off of him, somehow got to his feet, and he was off, racing around the other side of the house. Adam looked at her then at the man racing away.

"Go!" she said.

"Stay here," he commanded, then ran off after the man.

Margot's heart was thudding in her chest, trying to make sense of the situation. Who was the man? Had they somehow stepped in on a robbery? Had the man been watching the house and taken advantage of what he assumed was someone on vacation? But no, that seemed like too much of a coincidence. Then who was he?

Margot's mind raced back over the details of the case. Jerold had killed Mark Jennings for his grandson Thomas.

His grandson.

It was the only logical possibility, barring some random person just happening to be in this residence. And with that thought, her attention snagged on the now open back door.

She felt compelled to go inside, despite the fact that

Adam had told her to stay. Hands trembling, she told herself that the police were already on their way and it couldn't hurt to poke her head in, right?

Taking a silent breath, she went up the steps and paused at the backdoor. It led into what appeared to be a mudroom type area; two coats hung on the pegs and one pair of rubber boots sat under them.

She slipped past them and through an entryway that led into a galley type kitchen. It was relatively clean, but she noted two coffee mugs on the sink. Had Thomas been staying with his grandfather? That was one question she hadn't thought to ask the nosy neighbor. Had the woman seen Thomas enter the house?

Taking pains to make no sound, she walked to the end of the kitchen. The doorway opened to a hallway leading toward the front door with a living room along the right side. The TV reflected back a Food Network show, though the sound was on low. Her heart pounded in her chest as she stepped into the hallway. She took another step and was considering checking upstairs, before heading back out before the police arrived, when a hand clamped over her mouth.

Her heartbeat pounded in her ears but she resisted the urge to scream this time.

She felt like a fool. She should have stayed outside.

"Don't move," the voice said, close to her ear. She immediately recognized Jerold's voice, though he sounded even older than she remembered. She held up her hands to show him she meant him no harm.

"I'm going to let you talk, but I've got a needle right

here." The tip of a needle pricked the skin on her neck and everything in her body stiffened. She had to wait for the right moment. Mentally, she assessed how he was holding her, the leathery quality of his hand covering her mouth belied his age, and she knew in an instant she could easily get out of his grasp.

His hand slid down. "What do you want?"

She found it odd that he would ask such a question, but she wasn't going to take any chances.

"Jerold, it's me, Margot Durand."

She heard his quick intake of breath. "Wh-why are you here?"

Swallowing, she chose her words carefully. "I'm here with the police, Jerold. I think you know why we're here."

"Yeah? Well, where are they? Why'd they send you in? Last I heard, you were a baker."

He had her there. She affected a light laugh. "I'm working with them on this case," she fibbed, though it wasn't completely a lie. "But I wanted to come in to talk with you. To get your side of things. Why did you do it, Jerold?"

He stiffened but she thought he withdrew the needle, though she couldn't be sure.

"Do what?"

"I think you know."

She waited. She remembered Julian telling her that sometimes an interrogator's greatest weapon was silence.

"I had to."

Margot was shocked by this. Not just his admission,

but the complete and utter sadness that now infused his voice.

"What do you mean?"

The next instant, he'd shoved her away and was hovering near a chair opposite her, the needle held up to his own veins.

"Wait—Jerold, stop!"

Tears filled his eyes. "You don't understand. I—I couldn't stand to see my foolish grandson running with that Carow gang. His father made a mistake and I let him...but not with Thomas. He has such a promising future and he was throwing it away on drugs. I knew Victor's grandfather—we grew up together—and I arranged a deal with him. I promised to help him if Victor would release Thomas from his hold. Archie promised—he promised." Jerold sniffed, large tears falling down his face.

Margot's eyes stayed glued to the syringe, its tip pressing against the man's sun-spotted sink.

"Jerold, it's okay. We can talk this out—"

"It's not okay!" he said, his voice raising. "But I knew it." He was regaining his composure. "I knew I couldn't trust Archie or Victor. I made sure I had insurance, but now..." He looked up at her, a moment of clarity showing in his eyes. "Now it's of no use."

Then without another word or even a moment's hesitation, he shoved the syringe into his arm and depressed the plunger.

≈

THE NEXT FEW hours flew by faster than Margot thought possible. Unknown to her, Adam had come back from chasing Thomas, who was then safely in police custody, and he'd sneaked into the house behind Margot. He'd heard everything, capturing it on his phone's recording device, though he hadn't caught Jerold in time to stop the injection. It had happened too quickly.

Thankfully, the ambulance had already been called and they were briefed on the situation en route. With Adam's quick thinking, they had bagged the syringe and any other paraphernalia in the house so the ER techs would have something to work with.

Now, Margot sat in the hospital awaiting some sort of news. Adam was there as well, though he hadn't spoken more than a few words to her in as many hours.

"Detective Eastwood?" a doctor said, coming out of two double doors leading back to the ER.

"Yes?" Adam said, standing.

Margot did the same but didn't speak. She was distinctly aware of Adam's feelings and yet she was glad he'd allowed her to stay with him.

"It looks like you're in for a bit of good news, or at least I think it's good news."

"What's that, Doctor?" Adam said. He looked even more exhausted than that morning when Margot had first seen him at the park. His shirt was wrinkled, his hair messed, and the lines at the corners of his eyes looking deeper.

"Turns out there was no digoxin in Mr. Bascom's bloodstream. Instead, we found a massive dose of insulin.

He's a diabetic and I believe he was attempting to send himself into a diabetic coma. Fortunately, we were able to counteract that and he will make a full recovery. Though I am recommending a full suicide watch for at least the next few days, considering this information."

"Yes, yes, of course. We'll head up the security and watch for you. Thank you, Doctor."

The man nodded and left, and Adam went to speak with the officers who had stayed behind with him. He gave them instructions on what to do and then walked back to where Margot stood. The silence fell between them.

Margot looked up at Adam and saw relief along with exhaustion wash over him. It was over—or at least, mostly over. There was still one thing left for her to do.

"Adam," she said tentatively.

He looked down at her, but there was no anger there, merely exhaustion.

"I'm sorry. I shouldn't have gone into that house. It was foolish and—"

"It was," he said, turning to face her. Then he reached out and took her hands in his. "But I'm just glad you're safe."

She felt his forgiveness like a flood of cool water pouring over parched earth.

"I know you're inquisitive and I love that about you, but we've got to work on your listening skills."

She offered him a half-smile. "But I did get you your confession."

He rolled his eyes. "Good job, Watson."

"I still think I'm Sherlock," she said, winking at him.

"That remains to be seen." Then he stepped closer to her and she felt her pulse speed up. Thankfully, this time it had nothing to do with danger. Then again, was this danger of another kind?

"Margot, when all of this is over, could I take you to dinner?"

"Yes." Her response was immediate, but she wasn't afraid that she'd misspoken. In fact, she was certain she'd said exactly what she meant to. "I would like that, Detective Eastwood."

CHAPTER 16

THEY WALKED hand in hand through the gardens at *El Jardín*, a Spanish-style hacienda that offered its guests a unique dining opportunity near the banks of the Potomac. Rather than sit at a table and be served, guests made reservations in advance and, upon arrival, were given their own personal picnic meal, a bottle of wine made on the premises, and a blanket, then directed to a path that would take them through the gardens and to their reserved picnicking spot.

Margot had always wanted to visit *El Jardín,* but she'd never had the chance, until today and her first official date with the handsome detective.

While news of the high profile case that had come to North Bank was still circulating, it had been almost a month since Jerold's arrest. Though things were still far from being wrapped up, life in their small little town was slowly getting back to normal just in time for the fall season, but Margot wasn't sure if it would ever be the same.

"Here we are," Adam said, indicating a patch of grass under a sprawling oak tree. The weather was cooler, but Margot had come prepared with a heavier sweater and jeans. As she sat, sunlight spotting their blanket, she pulled the sweater on.

"Will it be too cold here?"

She shook her head. "It's perfect."

Adam held her gaze for a moment, as if assessing if she was telling the truth or not, then nodded once and unpacked the picnic basket.

They ate, discussing everything and anything, though she noticed he avoided his work and the case at all costs.

Finally, when she couldn't take it any longer, she put her wine glass down and narrowed her eyes at him. "Are you going to tell me what happened? Or do I need to drag it out of you, Detective Eastwood?"

"What are you talking about?" he said, coughing to cover his surprise at her direct words.

"I've hardly seen you since that day in the hospital and now you're avoiding any mention of the case. I'm curious. You know me better than that."

He grinned. "Not true. I saw you several times at the bakery."

"True," she consented, "but you spent most of the time talking with Dexter."

"How's that going by the way?"

"Well," she said, nodding. "He's a very competent assistant, though a little flamboyant on his desserts. A few years under my tutelage and he'll be a consummate professional, I'm sure." She laughed to show him she wasn't fully serious. "But really, he's a fantastic addition to the bakery."

"A permanent addition then?"

"I offered him a full-time position and he accepted. So yes." She took another sip. "But no changing the subject. What happened with Jerold and Thomas?"

"I can't imagine you haven't seen the news."

"I want the details. Nothing but the details."

"I knew you would."

She observed him but didn't see any disappointment on his features. It was more like resignation. He knew as well as she did that if this relationship was going to move forward, he would have to come to terms with the inquisitive nature of this French pastry chef.

"What I *can* tell you is that not all hope is lost."

"In what way?"

"Remember right before Jerold, uh—" Adam swallowed, looking like he'd rather be discussing anything but this. "—injected himself?"

"Yes, of course. He mentioned 'insurance.'"

"He did, and it's a good thing too. Now, you can't breathe a word of this to anyone—" Adam looked around then leaned closer. "—but he kept evidence he'd gotten from Mark before he killed him."

"What? How?"

"That's how he lured Mark to North Bank. He said he had more information for him and convinced him to come down to meet with him. Little did poor Mark know what he was getting himself into."

"But why wouldn't Mark just tell him to go to the police?"

"Jerold somehow convinced Mark that, at his age, he just wanted to live out a peaceful life. He said that Mark was already raking his name through the court system, why not take more information with him."

Margot nodded. It did make sense.

"Then comes George," Adam continued. "Apparently, before he went into painting full-time, Jerold worked at the bank were George used to make regular withdrawals. Add in some clever research and he had the perfect person to pin the murder on. With his access to Tamera's shop, it really was a good option—though thankfully, not error proof. We saw through the ruse pretty quickly, but some were almost convinced for a while there."

"Like you," she said, smirking.

He shrugged. "I go where the facts take me."

Then something else occurred to her. "Whatever happened to Harry?"

Now Adam leaned back and chuckled. "Poor Harry."

"You can't seriously mean that."

"I don't." Adam grew serious. "We caught him trying to leave town and have tried him for extortion, among other things. He'll spend some time in prison, that's for sure."

"I did talk with Tamera a few weeks ago and she said that George talked with Sarah and everything is out in the open now with no adverse effects. I suppose Harry is out of luck for blackmail in the future."

"Speaking of the future." Adam looked down at her and suddenly the stiff breeze did nothing to cool her heating cheeks. Something inside of her churned nervously and she looked down to fumble with the checkered blanket that they both sat on.

"Margot," Adam said, drawing her gaze back to his.

"Adam, I—"

"Would you like to go to the Fall Street Festival in D.C. with me next weekend?"

Immediately, her face filled with heat again. He was asking her to a street festival. Another date. Not...well, she wasn't sure what she'd thought he was going to say, but that wasn't important right now. Now that the danger was passed and her friend's husband was free, she could think of those *other* things.

And she did so now with a smile. "I'd love to."

He returned her smile as if he knew her internal struggle and was merely shaking his head at her leaping to conclusions, but all he said was, "Good. It's a date."

Thanks for reading *Desserts and Deception*. I hope you enjoyed reading the story as much as I enjoyed writing it. If you did, it would be awesome if you left a review for me on Amazon and/or Goodreads.

If you would like to know about future cozy mysteries by me and the other authors at Fairfield Publishing, make sure to sign up for our Cozy Mystery Newsletter. We will send you our FREE Cozy Mystery Starter Library just for signing up. All the details are on the next page.

As a special surprise, I have included a recipe for one of the treats that was featured in the book. You will find that recipe right after the newsletter information.

Lastly, at the very end of the book, I have included a couple previews of books by friends and fellow authors at Fairfield Publishing. First is a preview of *A Pie to Die For* by Stacey Alabaster - it's part of the popular Bakery Detectives Cozy Mystery series. Second is a preview of *Murder in the Mountains* by M. Lancaster. I really hope you like the samples. If you do, both books are available on Amazon.

- **FairfieldPublishing.com/pie-to-die-for**

- FairfieldPublishing.com/murder-in-mountains

FAIRFIELD COZY MYSTERY NEWSLETTER

Make sure you sign up for the Fairfield Cozy Mystery Newsletter so you can keep up with our latest releases. When you sign up, **we will send you our FREE Cozy Mystery Starter Library!**
   FairfieldPublishing.com/cozy-newsletter/

After you sign up to get your Free Starter Library, turn the page and check out the free previews :)

RECIPE

RELIGIEUSE

A RELIGIOUS IS a French pastry made up of two pastries filled with pastry cream, chocolate ganache and whip cream. This is not a quick and easy treat to make, but it will impress the heck out of anyone you serve them to :)

INGREDIENTS
- 60g/2¼oz butter, cut into cubes
- 75g/2½oz plain flour
- 2 free-range eggs, lightly beaten

FOR THE CRÈME pâtissière filling
- 500ml/18fl oz full-fat milk
- 1 vanilla pod, seeds only
- 6 medium free-range egg yolks
- 75g/2½oz caster sugar
- 20g/¾oz cornflour

• 25g/1oz plain flour

FOR THE CHOCOLATE ganache icing
• 150ml/5fl oz double cream
• 200g/7oz plain chocolate (around 36% cocoa solids) broken into pieces

FOR THE COLLAR
• 150ml/5fl oz double cream

RECIPE

1. Preheat the oven to 220C/425F/Gas 7. Line a baking tray with baking parchment and draw onto it eight circles 5cm/2in wide and another eight circles 2.5cm/1in wide. Put the butter in a heavy-based saucepan with 150ml/5fl oz of water and heat over a medium heat until the butter melts. Bring the mixture to the boil and then immediately remove from the heat.

2. Quickly tip in the flour. Stir vigorously with a wooden spoon until the mixture forms a soft ball. Return to the heat and cook over a low heat for 3-5 minutes, stirring constantly.

3. Remove from the heat and leave to cool slightly. Gradually add the eggs, beating well between each addition to form a smooth, shiny paste. Spoon the mixture into a piping bag fitted with a 1.5cm/ ½in plain nozzle.

4. Pipe round discs onto the baking tray in the marked circles and, using a damp finger, smooth over the top of each disc. Bake in the centre of the oven for 10 minutes. Reduce the oven temperature to 190C/375F/Gas 5 and cook for a further 10-15 minutes. Remove the choux buns from the oven and pierce each bun with a skewer to allow the steam to escape. Return to the oven for 4-5 minutes to dry out. Remove from the oven and leave to cool on a wire rack.

5. For the crème pâtissière filling, pour the milk and vanilla seeds into a heavy-based pan and bring gradually to the boil. Remove from the heat and leave to cool for 30 seconds. Meanwhile, in a medium bowl, whisk together the egg yolks and caster sugar until pale, then whisk in the cornflour and plain flour. Pour the vanilla-infused milk onto the eggs, whisking continuously, then pour back into the pan.

6. Bring back to the boil, whisking continuously over a medium heat and cook for one minute. Pour the crème pâtissière into a bowl. Cover the surface with cling film to prevent a skin from forming and leave to cool. Transfer to the fridge to chill.

7. For the chocolate ganache icing, bring the cream to the boil in a small pan. Remove from the heat. Add the chocolate and stir until melted and shiny. Transfer to a bowl and leave to cool. Transfer the fridge to chill until the ganache has thickened to a spreadable consistency.

8. To assemble the religieuse, spoon the cold crème pâtissière into a piping bag fitted with a long thin nozzle

(or alternatively you can use a jam syringe). Fill the choux buns with the crème pâtissière.

9. Dip the filled buns into the chocolate ganache to coat half-way up the sides. Sit the small buns on top of the larger buns.

10. For the collars, whip the cream in a mixing bowl until soft peaks form when the whisk is removed from the bowl. Spoon the cream into a piping bag fitted with a small star nozzle. Pipe lines of cream around the join where the small bun sits on top of the large bun to form a collar.

RECIPE SOURCE:

http://www.bbc.co.uk/food/recipes/religieuse_46431

PART I
BOOK PREVIEWS

PREVIEW: A PIE TO DIE FOR

"BUT YOU DON'T UNDERSTAND, I use only the finest, organic ingredients." My voice was high-pitched as I pleaded my case to the policeman. Oh, this was just like an episode of Criminal Point. Hey, I wondered who the killer turned out to be. I shook my head. That's not important, Rachael, I scolded myself. *What's important is getting yourself off this murder charge.* Still, I hoped Pippa had recorded the ending of the episode.

I tried to steady my breathing as Jackson—Detective Whitaker—entered the room and threw a folder on the table, before studying the contents as though he was cramming for a test he had to take the next day. He rubbed his temples and frowned.

Is he even going to make eye contact with me? Is he just going to completely ignore the interaction we had at the fair? Pretend it never even happened.

"Jackson..." I started, before I was met with a steely

glare. "Detective. Surely you can't think I had anything to do with this?"

Jackson looked up at me slowly. "Had you ever had any contact with Mrs. Batters before today?"

I shifted in my seat. "Yes," I had to admit. "I knew her a little from the store. She was always quite antagonistic towards me, but I'd never try to kill her!"

"Witnesses near the scene said that you two had an argument." He gave me that same steely glare. Where was the charming, flirty, sweet guy I'd meet earlier? He was now buried beneath a suit and a huge attitude.

"Well...it wasn't an argument...she was just...winding me up, like she always does."

Jackson shot me a sharp look. "So, she was annoying you? Was she making you angry?"

"Well... Well..." I tripped over my words. He was now making me nervous for an entirely different reason than he had earlier. Those butterflies were back, but now they felt like daggers.

Come on, Rach. Everyone knows that the first suspect in Criminal Point is not the one that actually did it.

But how many people had Jackson already interviewed? Maybe he was saving me for last. Gosh, maybe my cherry pie had actually killed the woman!

"Answer the question please, Miss Robinson."

"Not angry, no. I was just frustrated."

"Frustrated?" A smile curled at his lips before he pounced. "Frustrated with Mrs. Batters?"

"No! The situation. Come on—you were there!" I tried to appeal to his sympathies, but he remained a brick wall.

"It doesn't matter whether I was there or not. That is entirely besides the point." He said the words a little too forcefully.

I swallowed. "I couldn't get any customers to try my cakes, and Bakermatic was luring everyone away with their free samples." I stopped as my brows shot up involuntarily. "Jackson! Sorry, Detective. Mrs. Batters ate at Bakermatic as well!"

My words came out in a stream of breathless blabber as I raced to get them out. "Bakermatic must be to blame! They cut corners, they use cheap ingredients. Oh, and I know how much Mrs. Batters loved their food! She was always eating there. Believe me, she made that very clear to me."

Jackson sat back and folded his arms across his chest. "Don't try to solve this case for us."

I sealed my lips. *Looks like I might have to at this rate.*

"We are investigating every place Mrs. Batters ate today. You don't need to worry about that."

I leaned forward and banged my palm on the table. "But I do need to worry about it! This is my job, my livelihood...my life on the line. If people think I am to blame, that will be the final nail in my bakery's coffin!" Oh, what a day. And I'd thought it was bad enough that I hadn't gotten any customers at my stand. Now I was being accused of killing a woman!

I could have sworn I saw a flicker of sympathy finally crawl across Jackson's face. He stood up and readjusted his tie, but he still refused to make full eye contact. "You're free to go, Miss Robinson," he said gently. There was that tone from earlier, finally. He seemed recognizable as a human at long last.

"Really?"

He nodded. "For the moment. But we might have some more questions for you later, so don't leave town."

I tried to make eye contact with him as I left, squirreling out from underneath his arm as he held the door open for me, but he just kept staring at the floor.

Did that mean he wasn't coming back to my bakery after all?

Pippa was still waiting for me when I returned home later that evening. There was a chill in the air, which meant that I headed straight for a blanket and the fireplace when I finally crawled in through the door. Pippa shot me a sympathetic look as I curled up and crumbled in front of the flames. *How had today gone so wrong, so quickly?*

"I recorded the last part of the show," Pippa said softly. "If you're up for watching it."

I groaned and lay on the carpet, my back straight against the floor like I was a little kid. "I don't think I can stomach it after what I just went through. Can you believe it? Accusing ME of killing Mrs. Batters? When I *know* that Bakermatic is to blame. I mean, Pippa, they must be! But this detective wouldn't even listen to me when I was trying to explain Bakermatic's dodgy practices to him."

Pippa leaned forward and took the lid off a pot, the smell of the brew hitting my nose. "Pippa, what is that?"

She grinned and stirred it, which only made the smell worse. I leaned back and covered my nose. "Thought it might be a bit heavy for you. I basically took every herb, tea, and spice that you had in your cabinet and came up with this! I call it 'Pippa's Delight'!"

"Yeah well, it doesn't sound too delightful." I sat up and scrunched up my nose. "Oh, what the heck—pour me a cup."

"Are you sure?" Pippa asked with a cheeky grin.

"Go on. I'll be brave."

I braced myself as the brown liquid hit the white mug.

It was as disgusting as I had imagined, but at least it made me laugh when the pungent concoction hit my tongue. Pippa always had a way of cheering me up. If it wasn't her unusual concoctions, or her ever changing hair color—red this week but pink the last, and purple a week before that—then it was her never-ending array of careers and job changes that entertained me and kept me on my toes. When you're trying to run your own business, forced to be responsible day in and day out, you have to live vicariously through some of your more free-spirited friends. And Pippa was definitely that: free-spirited.

"Hey!" I said suddenly, as an idea began to brew in my brain. I didn't know if it was the tea that suddenly brought all my senses to life or what it was, but I found myself slamming my mug on the table with new found enthusiasm. "Pippa, have you got a job at the moment?" I could never keep up with Pippa's present state of employment.

She shrugged as she kicked her feet up and lay back on the sofa. "Not really! I mean, I've got a couple of things in the works. Why's that?"

I pondered for a moment. "Pippa, if you could get a job at Bakermatic, you could see first hand what they're up to!" My voice was a rush of excitement as I clapped my hands together. "You would get to find out the ways they cut corners, the bad ingredients they use, and, if you were really lucky, you might even overhear someone say something about Mrs. Batters!"

A gleam appeared in Pippa's green eyes. "Well, I do need a job, especially after today."

I raced on. "Yes! And you've got plenty of experience working in cafes."

"Yeah. I've worked in hundreds of places." She took a sip of the tea and managed to swallow it. She actually seemed to enjoy it.

"I know you've got a lot of experience. You're sure to get the job. They're always looking for part-timers." Unfortunately, Bakermatic was planning on expanding the storefront even further, and that meant they were looking for even more employees to fill their big yellow store. "Pippa, this is the perfect plan! We'll get you an application first thing in the morning. Then you can start investigating!"

Pippa raised her eyebrows. "Investigating?"

I nodded and lay my head back down on the carpet.

"Criminal Point—Belldale Style! Bakery Investigation Unit! I will investigate and do what I can from my end as well! Perhaps I could talk to people from all the other food stalls! Oh, Pippa, we're going to make a crack team of detectives!"

"The Bakery Detectives!"

We both started giggling but, as the full weight of the day's events started to pile up on me, I felt my stomach tighten. It might seem fun to send Pippa in to spy on Bakermatic, but this was serious. My bakery, my livelihood, and even my own freedom depended on it.

THANKS FOR READING a sample of my book, *A Pie to Die For*. I really hope you liked it. You can read the rest at:

FairfieldPublishing.com/pie-to-die-for

OR YOU CAN GET it for free by signing up for our newsletter.

FairfieldPublishing.com/cozy-newsletter/

MAKE sure you turn to the next page for the preview of *Murder in the Mountains*.

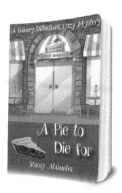

FairfieldPublishing.com/pie-to-die-for

PREVIEW: MURDER IN THE MOUNTAINS

Screams were not a normal part of the workday at Aspen Breeze. When Jennifer heard the anguished cry of the maid, she ran around the desk and sprinted out the door. Clint, not through with his breakfast, followed at her heels. The door to the room had been left open. The maid stood on the thick burgundy carpet in front of the unmade bed and pointed at the hot tub.

Water remained in the tub, but it wasn't swirling. The occupant, a red-haired, slightly chubby man whose name Jennifer had forgotten, was face down. His blue running shorts had changed to a darker blue due to dampness. Reddish colorations marred his throat. Another dark spot of blood mixed with hair around his right temple. Pale red splotches marred the water.

For a moment, she felt like the ground had opened and she had fallen into blackness. Legs weakened. Knees buckled. She shook her head and a few incoherent syllables came from her mouth. Clint's arm grasped her around her waist.

"Step back. It's okay," he said.

It was a silly thing to say, he later thought. Clearly, it was not okay, but in times of stress people will often say and do stupid things.

He eased her backward, and then sat her down on the edge of the bed. He walked back and took a second look at the hot tub. He had seen dead bodies when he covered the police beat. It wasn't a routine occurrence, but he had stood in the rain twice and on an asphalt pavement once as EMTs covered a dead man and lifted him into an ambulance.

By the time he turned around, Jennifer was back on her feet and the color had returned to her cheeks.

She patted her maid on the shoulder. "Okay, it's all right. We have to call the police. You can go, Maria. Go to the office and lay down."

"Yes, ma'am."

She glanced at Clint and saw he had his cell phone out.

"...at the Aspen Breeze Lodge," he was saying. "There's a dead body in Unit Nine. It doesn't look like it was a natural death." He nodded then slipped the cell phone in his pocket. "They said the chief was out on a call but should be here within fifteen minutes."

"Good." Jennifer put her hands on her hips. Her gaze stared toward the hot tub. A firm, determined tone came back in her voice.

"Clint, those marks on his throat. The red on his forehead. This wasn't an accident, was it?"

"We can't really say for sure. He might have tripped and hit…." The words withered in the face of her laser stare. "I doubt it. I…I really can't say for sure but…I doubt it."

They looked at one another for a few seconds. Light yellow flames rose up from the artificial fireplace and the crackling of wood sounded from the flames. Jennifer sighed. She realized there was nothing to do except wait for the police.

The silence was interrupted by a tall, thin man, unshaven as yet, who rushed in.

"Bill, what are you doing with the door open? It's still cold…." He stopped as if hit by a stun gun. Eyes widened. He stumbled but caught himself before he fell to the carpeted floor. "Oh, no! What happened?"

Jennifer shifted into her professional tone as manager. "We don't know yet, sir. I assume you knew this man."

He nodded weakly. "Yeah, Bill's been a friend of mine for years."

"I remember you from when you checked in yesterday, but I'm sorry I can't remember your name."

"Dale Ramsey."

Ramsey had a thin, pale face that flashed even paler. There was a chair close to him and he collapsed in it. He had an aquiline nose and chin but curly brown hair. His hand went to his heart.

"Sorry you had to learn about your friend's death this way, Mr. Ramsey," Jennifer said. "I regret to say I've forgotten his name too."

"Bill Hamilton."

Jennifer turned back to Clint. "Do you think we should move the body? Put it on the rug and cover it with a blanket?"

Clint shook his head. "I think the police would prefer it stay right where it is, at least for now."

Jennifer nodded. A steel gaze came in her eyes. She looked at Ramsey, who almost flinched. Then he shook slightly as if dealing with the aftermath of a panic attack.

"Mr. Ramsey, I am the owner of this Lodge and obviously I am very upset someone used it as a place for murder. So I trust you won't mind if I ask you a few questions - just to aid the police, of course."

Ramsey swallowed, or tried to. It looked like a rock had lodged in his throat. "Of course not. I...I do will anything I can to help," he said.

"Six single individuals checked into my lodge last night. That's a little unusual. I was commenting on that to Clint just last night. Now it turns out that you knew the deceased. Do you know the other four people who checked in?"

"Yes...I...yes."

There was a pause and Jennifer noted the look of sadness in his eyes.

"I realize you are upset, Mr. Ramsey, so just relax and take your time."

"We are all members of the Centennial Historical Society. All of us are history buffs," he finally answered.

"Why did you all check in here?"

Ramsey shifted in his chair. "This may sound unbelievable."

"Let's try it and see," Jennifer said.

"About a hundred and twenty-five years ago there was a Wells Fargo gold shipment in these parts. An outlaw gang headed by a man nicknamed The Falcon stole it. He got the name because he liked heights and the Rocky Mountains and had actually trained a falcon at one time. Rumor is, the gang got about a hundred thousand worth in gold, coins and bars. What's known is the gang drifted apart and a few members got shot, but the gold was never found. We believe it's buried very close by, up in the Rocky Mountain National Forest."

Jennifer nodded. The entrance to the forest was less than five miles from Aspen Breeze. All drivers had to do was turn left when they left the lodge and they would hit the entrance in about ten minutes.

"The Rocky Mountain National Forest is a huge area, thousands of miles there of virtually unexplored wilderness. You better have a specific location or you'll spend your lifetime looking and never find anything," she said.

'We have researched this gang for years. We think we know approximately where the gold was buried. It's more than just recovering the gold. This would be a historical find of enormous significance. We were going up there today to try to find the site."

"Maybe someone didn't want to share," Clint said.

Ramsey shook his head. "I doubt it. I've known these people for years. I don't think anyone would kill Bill. Besides, whoever it was would have to kill all of us too if he wanted to keep the gold to himself. Bill was in the high tech field, lower management, but he also liked the wilderness. He knew this forest better than any of us. We were counting on him to help find the site of the gold. He had searched the forest a number of times during the past five years.

I came out with him a few times. He thought he knew where the outlaws had hid their stash. He shared his opinions with us, but he was the one with the most expertise. Eddie, Eddie Tercelli, one of our group, is the second most knowledgeable about the location. He was out a few times too with Bill searching. But it would be tough for him to find the place on his own."

A blue light waved and flickered in the room. They heard a car door open and then slam shut. They looked up as the officer walked in. He wore a fine, crisp blue uniform with a bright silver badge. He had a slight paunch over his belt, but it didn't make him look old or slow. The intense gray eyes under the rim of the black police cap took in everything. His revolver was clearly visible on his right hip.

"Chief Sandish," Clint said, nodding.

Thanks for reading a sample of my first book, *Murder in the Mountains*. I really hope you liked it. It is available on Amazon at:

FairfieldPublishing.com/murder-in-mountains

Oʀ ʏᴏᴜ ᴄᴀɴ ɢᴇᴛ it for free by signing up for our newsletter.

FairfieldPublishing.com/cozy-newsletter/

FairfieldPublishing.com/murder-in-mountains